Tam[illegible]

My [illegible]
about inner [illegible]
inspire you [illegible]
visions! Best
Wishes!

[illegible signature]

Zlavik

by
Peter Jarrett

Bloomington, IN

Milton Keynes, UK

AuthorHouse™
1663 Liberty Drive, Suite 200
Bloomington, IN 47403
www.authorhouse.com
Phone: 1-800-839-8640

AuthorHouse™ UK Ltd.
500 Avebury Boulevard
Central Milton Keynes, MK9 2BE
www.authorhouse.co.uk
Phone: 08001974150

First published by AuthorHouse 12/13/2006

ISBN: 1-4208-5221-3 (sc)

Printed in the United States of America
Bloomington, Indiana

This book is printed on acid-free paper.

For T.C.

But every man is more than just himself; he also represents the unique... and remarkable point at which the world's phenomenon intersect, only once in this way and never again. This is why every man's story is important, eternal, sacred; this is why every man as long as he lives... is wondrous and worthy of every consideration. In each individual the spirit becomes flesh, in each man the creation suffers, within each man the redeemer is crucified to the cross...

I have been and still am a seeker but I have ceased to question stars and books; I have begun to listen to the teachings my blood whispers to me.

Herman Hesse, *Demian*

Acknowledgements

A variety of talented people gave me valuable support and encouragement in the writing of this book. First, I received important editing and consultation assistance from Kelly Conway and Mark Wisniewski. Also important, through the many revisions of this book, was the steadfast word processing services of Barbara Allen.

A variety of readers gave me important feedback and encouragement: Alex and Nina Herlihy, Celeste Jarrett, Cindy Jarrett and Jennifer Rakvin.

A special thanks is given to Joyce Corinna, my wife, whose unflinching and unconditional support of this ten year project helped immeasurably.

CHAPTER 1

The junkyard was owned by Justin P. Samuels, a gaunt, silver haired man with a bad limp, who lived in a shack near the entrance gate. He lived alone, except for three huge, vicious German Shepherds. Everyone knew that Samuels beat the dogs.

I was twelve and building a tree house several hundred feet behind the junkyard itself. I hoped all my building materials would be free—courtesy of Justin Samuels. I'd access the junkyard by digging a hole under the fence, which I covered with brush. I learned that a good time to sneak into the junkyard was after school, when the dogs were chained and Samuels was in his shack.

"Martin," I said one afternoon, "I need help getting a door from the junkyard." My older brother never said 'no' to me, and he knew I was afraid of dogs.

"We should have a plan in case the dogs are loose," Martin said. I told him there was an old, green 1950 Ford Sedan halfway between the fence opening and the pile of lumber, and we agreed that he'd jump in the car if he were chased.

On the following Friday, he crawled through the hole and checked out the car. The driver's door opened, and the windows were still intact. He climbed inside, closed the door, made a face at me, then gave me the thumbs-up sign and I laughed and waved. Martin then got out of the car and strutted to the pile of lumber and yanked free a door, walked back and pushed it over the top of the fence to where I was waiting. He slid through the hole, whacked the dirt off his jeans and grinned. "Dad would give us hell for this," he laughed.

I paused. "Are you afraid of the dogs?"

"I'll whip into that Ford and make faces at them if they show up." Martin pretended to cuff me on the shoulder. "Don't worry, Bro."

The following week, I'd spotted two new doors in Samuel's ever-changing collection. I could complete the tree house. "Martin?" I said, "this Sunday can you help--one more time?"

He sighed, "Sure."

There was one problem. Samuels had a habit of leaving the junkyard and driving off for a few hours every Sunday afternoon. His practice was to untie the shepherds while he was away. The dogs would stay near the shack unless they heard a noise. I forgot to tell Martin about this until the last minute.

We left for the junkyard after church. Martin let me strap on the Bowie knife that he'd bought at Bernie's Pawn Shop, but he waited until we were on the outskirts of town before he handed it to me. I slid the long, dark, brown leather sheath with its fifteen-inch knife on my belt feeling a jolt of pride. Martin said I could keep the knife at my fort, but, he made me swear I wouldn't slip by mentioning the knife to our parents.

At the hole in the fence, I said, "We've got to be careful--it's Sunday afternoon--the dogs could be loose."

"Hey, bro, you'd save me with that knife—right?" I nodded and swallowed at the same time.

Martin crawled through the hole and strolled towards the pile of lumber. He patted the green Ford's hood at the halfway point, as if to reassure himself. He was at the lumber pile within two minutes, and started to wiggle a door loose from the heap, when one of the dogs barked. Martin stopped and cupped his hand to his ear, until the barking stopped.

He then went back to the door, pulling it back and forth. He had the door all but a foot out when the rumbling began. Lumber on top of the pile had shifted, triggering a roaring avalanche. The dogs began barking.

"Run for it!" I yelled.

Martin faced the direction of the barking dogs, his hands still squeezing the door.

"Martin... Run!" I shouted.

He turned, dropped the door and began to run the two hundred feet to the opening. I spotted one of the dogs entering the area heading for Martin.

"Go to the car!" I screamed. "There's a dog!"

Martin bolted for the Ford which was a hundred feet away. The dog was sixty feet away and closing.

The second and third dogs appeared as Martin crashed into the side of the Ford. Next he was pulling and kicking the door. "Jesus Christ, he yelled as the handle came off in his hand.

"Go *under* the car," I screamed but the first dog jumped on Martin's back and threw him to the ground. I watched as the two other dogs hurled themselves on my brother. One tore into Martin's leg while the other two were at his torso. Martin was kicking and hitting the dogs as he thrashed about.

"Allen," he shrieked, "the knife!"

This isn't happening, I thought. I wanted to help my brother but couldn't move.

Martin did manage to stand up once. His shirt was in shreds and he was streaming blood from multiple wounds, but the dogs pulled him down. There was one final sound from Martin, a horrible wail like the sound a rabbit makes before it dies.

I ran down the road that led from the junkyard to town and had run several hundred feet when I saw a car coming. I cut on to the yellow lines waving my hands wildly.

The car stopped--it was Justin Samuels.

"Your dogs are killing my brother!"

Samuels raced his car down the road driving right through the chain link gate.

"Please, God, make Martin all right!" Everything was blurry in my head as I ran propelled by blind instinct. I'd felt myself turn into a Cheetah—the fastest thing alive. My speed doubled. My house was getting closer.

I tore off the flimsy screen door as I flew into the living room where Mom and Dad were reading the Sunday papers.

"The dogs are killing Martin...the dogs are killing him." I added Samuels junkyard.

Dad ran to his car and raced out of the driveway throwing up a small plume of gravel in his wake. Mom called the police who told her that Samuels had already called. She then got me a glass of water, and told me to calm myself. I sat down in Dad's brown leather chair trying to sip water while I repeated to myself that Martin would be okay. My mother paced the room, back and forth, lighting up one cigarette after another which she alternated with looking out the window. Officer Irving drove Dad home in the cruiser and the other officer followed in Dad's car. The police told my mother that Martin's trachea had been punctured and he'd bled to death. Officer Irving had shot all three dogs. My father, who was sobbing, had gone into the bathroom.

Mom put out her last cigarette after the police left. My father came out of the bathroom, his right eye was twitching, and he was still crying. He kept muttering "Martin was everything...he was everything." Mom took Dad into his study and gave me a funny look before she closed the doors. I went upstairs to my room. I remembered the Bowie knife and I took it off my belt and hid the weapon in my bottom drawer under a Monopoly game.

We held the service for Martin on the following Saturday; the funeral was closed casket. The church was overflowing for Dad was the minister of the largest protestant church in town, not to mention everyone knew Martin. Almost all of the sophomore class was there.

Mrs. Thomas, Martin's English teacher, spoke, reading an essay Martin had written after he heard Dad give a sermon on Cain and Abel. The essay was entitled, "My Brother's Keeper." I blanked on what it was all about.

All through the service I felt frozen like I had when the dogs were attacking Martin. At the end I stood with Mom and Dad at the entrance doors and acknowledged everyone as they left. My brown corduroy suit felt tight.

Some people hesitated when they shook my hand. Afterwards, Reverend Bill Larson, the Baptist minister, ushered me into the vestibule and grabbed me by both shoulders. "Son, don't go blaming yourself--it was none of your doing." I nodded but looked away.

Two weeks later Dad put a lock on Martin's door. Everything in Martin's room was kept exactly as it had been including his unmade bed, dirty clothes, and the open geometry book on his desk. Neither of my parents gave an explanation.

A week later Dad came upstairs to my room. He had a tight look on his face. "Was there anything different you could've done when the dogs attacked Martin?"

"No." My voice broke. "The dogs were too big and they'd have killed me...everything happened so fast."

Dad looked at me for a long time. "I have to accept what happened as God's will." His voice sounded flat.

I never cried at Martin's funeral. During the following week, I felt that while I slept someone was injecting me, over and over, with shots from a massive Novocain needle. Once at dinnertime, Dad mentioned Martin's name, and I started choking, and he had to whack me on the back--hard--a number of times.

I had a recurring dream being with Martin at Samuels' Junkyard. Martin was being attacked by the dogs and he kept signaling for me to bring the knife. I'd crawl under the fence and run towards him, but I'd hit an invisible, thick, glass wall. I'd pound, kick and slam, but couldn't get through. Martin's screams were silent and his eyes bulged as the dogs pulled him down.

Dad sent me to see a psychiatrist. Dr. Milliken wore dark-rimmed glasses, sat behind a black desk, and didn't say much. All he did was nod and write on a yellow pad. I told Dad I didn't want to go anymore. He said it was okay. I overheard him tell Mom he was glad because the fees were high.

Exactly one year after my brother's death, I noticed the lock was off his door. Dad was inside sitting on the bed, his hands covering his face, crying.

I walked away. Later that night, while Mom and Dad were asleep, I took the Bowie knife out of my drawer, and brought it up to the attic, and hid it under a loose floor board by the chimney.

CHAPTER 2

Dad had been the minister of the Greenfield Congregational Church for fifteen years. The church was quintessential New England: white clapboards, four pillars in front, and a tall steeple. The building was located in the center of town facing the town green. We lived in the parsonage next to the church. Our house was a three story, white clapboard, Victorian, with a Mansard slate roof; both Martin and I were born there. Everyone in the family liked the house except Dad.

My mother, Beth Ford, loved the house. Every year she had a major painting or wallpapering job going on. She had fixed up a room on the second floor as an office to correct her papers and do crafts. She was a fourth grade teacher at the elementary school. Mom was pretty and smart but sometimes I heard people say she was stand-offish. Once at a church rummage sale I overheard two women comment as my mother walked in, "Here she comes now--June Cleaver on ice."

My parents had few arguments but once I overheard one about how my father treated me. I was outside of Dad's study and I overheard my mother. "I need to talk to you about the boys."

I heard a rustle of the paper followed by a long sigh as my father put down his paper.

"You're still favoring Martin."

My father didn't say anything for a few seconds. "I don't buy it," said my father, raising his voice.

"You should see how you look at Martin at the dinner table when he talks." Mom then mentioned how Dad bought a new winter coat for Martin even though I was the one who needed it. "You took Martin and his friends to the Enfield Fair on his birthday--Allen had only a party."

I pressed closer to the shut pocket doors. There was an illicit thrill going through me at hearing Mom speak up for me.

"We must face facts." My father cleared his throat. "Martin is so much more gifted—–intelligence, personality and athletic ability. Those gifts require extra attention. Allen is in a different league."

"You need to treat them equally."

"I don't see a problem. The boys are fine the way things are." My father walked towards the doors. I moved down the hall towards the kitchen--fast.

Every winter Martin and I built a huge snow fort. We always named it Fort Banner because my brother would find one of Mom's old scarves, tie it to a stick and use as our flag. On our last winter, we instead, built a huge snow mountain. We took three days shoveling and shaping the snow into a huge mound. We decided to tunnel in from opposite ends and meet in the middle. The next day was spent digging in from opposite ends. We were excited because we could hear each others chopping sounds.

At frequent intervals, we kept signaling through muffled yells. Martin's fist was the first to puncture the wall. We both grabbed each other's arms and yelled a war whoop as our hands clasped.

Martin told me about his special tree when I was eleven. He had discovered a hundred foot high beech tree on the north side of town in an area that had a marsh and was avoided by most people.

"Allen, the tree must be three hundred years old and it would take four kids to circle their arms around the trunk." Martin said he discovered it when he was twelve; he also said he freed the tree, cleaned out the undergrowth, and vines. He kept the tree his secret for over two years before he showed it to me.

Martin said he'd lie down on one of the lower branches draping himself like a cat on the back of a sofa; once he even fell asleep on the branch. He said on warm days he could even sense when the sap was running. Martin said the tree had a woman's spirit. "I swear she talks to me."

My brother worried about the tree during high winds and winter storms. Several times he came into my room at two or four in the morning and asked me if I thought the tree would be okay. I would groan and plead with him to leave me alone. He'd apologize and go back to his room.

One morning I felt an ice-coated stick being rubbed in my face. "Bro, this is from the tree--you gotta see it." The time was eight, Saturday morning. Martin knew I loved to sleep in and catch the late morning cartoons.

He said an ice storm had coated every branch and limb. "Bro, it is the most amazing thing I've ever seen--c'mon, get dressed, ya gotta check it out." Martin made me hustle before the sun started to melt things.

We arrived at the site an hour later. There were no clouds and the sun was hitting the spot directly. The tree was like a crystal-coated giant sculpture with hundreds of spiraling elongated arms, each one with hands and fingers. Every branch, limb and twig was shimmering and reflecting in the morning sunlight. The beech tree was like a queen of nature draped with thousands of sparkling jewels.

The two of us stood there, in silence for a long time. There were no sounds except the occasional tinkling-like chimes of tiny ice coated twigs falling from the weight of the ice. We were the only witnesses.

I got it that morning: Martin knew secrets that others didn't know. We walked back to the house in single file, without saying anything. There was just the sound of our boots crunching through the thick crusted snow. We walked in an easy rhythm shielding our eyes from the bright sunlight. On that morning I could feel some kind of invisible wire burrowing into me from Martin.

In January of 1961 our family watched John F. Kennedy take the oath of office and give his inaugural address on a snowy Saturday afternoon. Martin turned to me afterwards. "Bro, that speech will be famous--I know it." Dad didn't say much, he'd voted for Nixon.

Martin started a scrapbook on Kennedy in the following months filling the album with pictures and articles about the new president. I'd help him by cutting and trimming the stories before he would paste them. He filled up one album within a year. On Friday, November 22, 1963, Martin and I were home with colds. Martin flipped on the TV around one o'clock.

I saw a terrible look on his face as I walked into the room. "Oh my god! Oh my god!" he held his head and repeated the line a number of times, after Walter Cronkite announced that President Kennedy had been assassinated.

Dad, Mom, Martin and I were hooked to the TV for the next three days. My brother said very little until he saw Jack Ruby shoot Oswald. He yelled out "What's happening to our country?" Later that night at supper, he had a dark look on his face. "The whole thing shouldn't have happened," he said several times at the dinner table.

One week later Martin announced that he wanted to go into politics and become a senator. Mom and Dad said encouraging things and Dad made a joke by asking Martin to promise him he'd stay a Republican.

In early Spring, Martin came into my room at dawn. He whispered my name several times while poking me on the shoulder.

"Hey Bro...wake-up...Bro."

"Huh?"...I was rubbing my eyes.

"Bro, I had an amazing dream!"

"What?" It felt like the middle of the night.

He grabbed me on both shoulders. "I gotta tell you about my dream, Bro, c'mon."

"Martin, leave me alone, I wanna go back to sleep."

"Just listen, huh." Martin grabbed my hands and pulled me up like I was some Jack-in-the-box.

"My dream was too weird to tell Mom and Dad." He began pacing back and forth alongside my bed. He'd just turned fifteen and I could see where his chest was filling out and a stubble of beard was beginning to show on his chin and over his lip.

He explained that he was hanging out by his tree when he saw an adult man wearing Chinos and a dark blue polo shirt walking towards him. He said the man was smiling and waving at him--it was Jack Kennedy. JFK signaled Martin to sit down next to him on a nearly fallen tree and began a conversation.

President Kennedy said a plan was surfacing that would cause things in the world to move faster. He told Martin special young people around the world were being chosen to spearhead the change. My brother was one of them.

Martin sat back down again on my bed. "I can't believe I've been picked for this!" He said Kennedy showed him a high speed movie of how the world was going to shift in the next fifty years.

"You won't believe it Bro! All the changes that are coming-so many new inventions, changes in governments, social upheavals and wars. "Bro, there is enough wealth for everyone. There doesn't have to be poor people. The seven Baylor kids don't have to live in that rust-bucket trailer over on Turner Street. Everything can be so much better."

"Martin, it was only a dream!" I was irritated with my brother's enthusiasm at six in the morning.

"Allen it was real!" My brother had shouted to me with a new, stern look. He said it was like a tuning fork inside of him had begun vibrating. "I can still feel the hum."

"Why are you telling me this?"

"Kennedy mentioned your name. He said you'd be my partner just like Bobby was for him. Crazy huh?"

Martin started hitting me with the pillow and laughing. He quieted down and said he was going to study his head off through high school and get into a great college. "Then I'll go to law school and someday be a governor or senator with the power to start the plan."

I shook my head.

"Bro...the dream was real." He was smiling, crying, and laughing—all at the same time.

I felt a strong jolt entering me from the invisible wire that connected me to my brother. I decided, somehow, that I would find a way to accept Martin's dream.

During the next few weeks Martin kidded, or joked with me like never before. I loved the idea of being partners with him like Jack and Bobby Kennedy. During this time, I could feel the wire humming like something was permanently flowing between us.

In the years that followed my brother's death I tried to hang on to Martin's dream but I could sense it fading. I would go to his tree at least once a month and stand there in silence. I hungered for the certainty of the hum and vibration of the tuning fork. Once I even draped myself on the tree as Martin had, but nothing happened. The tree didn't seem special—just a big, dumb object whose secrets, if any, were dormant. Without my brother, it was hard to believe in magical trees, dreams or special missions.

CHAPTER 3

It wasn't until high school that I began to think less about Martin's death. One Sunday afternoon, in late October, I took a long walk to Two Mile Pond where Martin and I had swam as kids; it was midday and cold despite the fall sun. I sat on a rock ledge that we'd used as a diving board. I threw pebbles into the water, and took comfort in watching the flat sheen of the water break into endless, radiating ripples.

I was edgy. The previous Wednesday would've been Martin's eighteenth birthday. Mom, Dad and myself were quiet all day. Yet something stirred and pushed against the metal band that now bracketed my chest. The thought came to me: "Make something that reminds you of two brothers." I looked at the nearby brook that flowed from the pond. Martin had said it flowed to the ocean. I found two sticks and tied them together with a weed I found near the shore. I dropped the sticks into the brook and watched it as it wove, bobbed and bounced off different rocks, then disappeared.

Maybe the sticks would reach Europe or Africa. Maybe a kid would find them. I was lighter as I walked home, and reminded myself about the ripples that went on forever, as well as the bound sticks that were heading for the ocean. However, the restless feeling came back as I ate supper with my parents that night. And the metal band began to tighten again.

My education about girls accelerated during high school. We met in the Pilgrim Fellowship Church youth group. We were Co-Chairmen during that year, and somehow, fell into going steady. Her name was Gladys Williams.

She was a popular, cute and cheerful girl, and her father was President of the Greenfield Community Bank. Her family had a huge Tudor style house with a pool—in the wealthiest part of town. I could tell she liked me because throughout ninth grade, she would sit next to me at the fellowship meetings.

However, Gladys provided a major log jam for exploring the ways of the flesh. When I tried to kiss her, she would turn her head to make sure I kissed her cheek. If we slow-danced, her whole body would go rigid. The only thing I could do was hold hands with her, but not around our parents.

My frustration grew worse when my friend, Jimmy Bratton bragged about his make-out sessions with his girlfriend. "Hey, sounds like Gladys would make a great minister's daughter." Jimmy would always laugh first and loudest.

My friend Ollie (who stuttered) didn't help matters either. "Why d-d-don't you read the dirty passages in the Bible," he'd say, "that could get her t-t-turned on."

I was fond of Ollie. We'd gone to school together since the first grade, and had always been in the same class through sixth grade. I spent a lot of time with him because he only lived a few blocks away. He was short, with a body like a dwarf, and was a stutterer. Ollie was always thanking me for not making fun of how he talked. However, he could, at times be jealous of Gladys.

I didn't want to give up on Gladys. My plan for the big move on her was our date for the Halloween Dance. I had reviewed my strategy with Ollie and Jimmy. They both approved. I would take Gladys to the bluff at Blairs Falls, the local lovers' lane. I bought both new shaving lotion and a shirt.

We left the dance at ten. I told Gladys I had a mystery ride for her, and when I arrived and removed the blindfold, she shrieked.

"This is Blairs Falls! We shouldn't be here."

"I thought we could enjoy the view."

"This is a place where couples make-out. It's bad for our reputations."

"Who's going to know?"

"People will recognize your father's car. They'll talk."

"Why can't we just kiss?"

"Your father is my minister!"

"We're not in church--he isn't here!"

"We're in his car and you're his son!" Gladys folded her arms and glared. "I can't believe you brought me here."

"I want to kiss you!"

"We're Co-chairs of the Greenfield Pilgrim Youth Fellowship!"

"Jesus," I muttered.

"What did you say?"

"Jesus," I said calmly.

"You're taking the Lord's name in vain."

"Gladys, Congregationalists are allowed to use the Lord's name in vain--it's the Baptists who can't."

"I don't believe you."

"I know about this-–after all, I'm the minister's son."

"You're acting crazy--take me home right now."

I threw the car in reverse, spun a tight circle, and raced away from the bluff.

Gladys and I called a truce a week later. We agreed to continue going steady until the Junior Prom. I felt as if I were in an arranged marriage. We broke-up that June after agreeing to remain friends. I dated several other girls that year but, there was always something missing.

CHAPTER 4

Millard Fillmore College was an obscure liberal arts college of eleven hundred students located in upstate New York. My parents took me on my initial visit. My father was enthusiastic because of their scholarship for a student preparing for the ministry. Our first view of the campus was appealing as we entered a valley from the south and saw the small town of Upton, New York nestled against a backdrop of mountains. A tall clock tower rose from the middle of the campus. The effect was pleasant except for the acrid smell from the smoke stacks of a paper mill at the north end of town.

Our student guide, Matt, gave the history of the eccentric farmer founder who started the college. He said Abner Townsend was born in 1810 into a poor family of eleven children. He was a bachelor all his life, worked hard, saved his money, and bought, acre by acre, all the adjoining farms. He also acquired a general store and a sawmill. Abner's hero was Millard Fillmore, who then was the local Congressman. Upon Townsend's death, all his money went to start a college named after the renowned, underachieving, thirteenth President of the United States.

Matt walked with us in silence for awhile and then lit up with his final comment. "Oh, the main academic building with the huge clock tower was named after him--Townsend Towers." Matt pointed to the huge tower. "The building is the symbol for the college."

"What a generous man," my mother said.

Matt laughed. "Well, there're stories that he was a little weird."

"Weird?" My mother looked puzzled.

"Well, ah, the rumor was that he was...ah unusually close to his animals--especially his sheep."

"Oh." My mother's forehead started wrinkling.

Matt winked at my father.

"Young man, tell us about the extracurricular activities."

Matt mentioned the different clubs and shared a tip about dorm assignments. "Avoid the third floor of Laher Hall," he said.

I told Ollie Brown about my visit, and we shared a bevy of doubts.

"Je-Je-Je-Jesus...it's strange they named a college after Fillmore." Ollie said he'd done a research paper on Fillmore for U.S. History. Fillmore had become an accidental president when Taylor died in office in 1850, he explained. At the next convention, his own party didn't nominate him. Four years later, Fillmore ran as the presidential candidate of a reactionary group called the "Know-Nothing Party."

My acceptance letter came in early April, informing me that I'd been awarded the four-year ministry scholarship. I'd major in liberal arts as my preparation for the ministry. The scholarship was endowed by Abner Townsend, the friend of presidents, ministers-to-be, and sheep.

My father puffed on his pipe as he drove me to campus for freshman year. "Shame Martin never got his chance. God knows he could've become someone extraordinary." He sighed and I stiffened against my seat. Several hours later we had pulled up in front of my dorm.

My dorm room was on the third floor of Laher Hall. I liked my roommate Shaun McAdams, who was from a small town in Connecticut, like me. He was small and wiry with a large head and a big smile. He reminded me of a young leprechaun. After he and I met, he closed the door and turned to me with a solemn look. "Hey, Ford, turns out we're the only freshmen on a floor of upper classmen, most of the basketball team lives on this floor and some of them look like they just learned to walk upright." He got down on all fours and began to grunt and scurry back and forth.

The students were a mixed bag of liberal arts and teacher education majors. The most popular major was physical education. I took an immediate dislike to Larry Erskine, the reigning star of the basketball team who lived two doors down at the end of the hallway. Erskine was six feet, six inches in height. His lanky body and small head made him look like an upright praying mantis with a permanent idiot's grin. He played center for the basketball team and averaged twenty-five points a game. His major pastime was to spend several hours every night throwing coat hangers down the hall to hit the door of his soul brother.

The object of his affection was "Ty-Ty" Hapgood who was the star forward of the team. "Ty-Ty" was six four with wide, hulking shoulders. He had close-cropped hair, a small forehead with bead-like eyes and a protruding jaw. In fact, his nickname within the team was "Nean." No one outside the team was allowed to call him that.

"Ty-Ty" was also renowned for his foul breath. He had tried everything to eliminate it, but it persisted. He did find one constructive use. In the previous year's championship game, during a foul shot, he was seen to have bent forward and breathed on the shooter's face and the shooter missed.

Larry and Ty-Ty would usually play coat-hanger-throw every evening between eight and twelve. The object of the game was to hit the door of the opponent two times in a row without being caught.

Because of their brawn no one in Laher complained. Students who used the hallway at night would squish their backs up against the walls and cover their faces to avoid the inevitable fusillade of hangers.

I became irritated by the game. I typed an anonymous letter, taped a matchbook to it, and slid it under Ty-Ty's door.

> Dear Ty-Ty:
>
> This is called a match book. If you remove one of these cardboard sticks with the red tip and rub it fast against the rough black stripe, it will spark and create something called fire. Now that you have this secret you can go home to your cave and raise your family.
>
> Taylor Tyler
> President, Millard Fillmore College

Later that evening Ty-Ty pounded on our door and threw it open. "Hey, frosh, you know anything about this?" He threw the letter on Shaun's desk.

Shaun read the letter and shook his head. "Sounds pretty sick to me."

"Yeah, some sick fucker is trying to pull shit on me. I'll fix 'em good."

Ty-Ty scanned both our faces for several moments, then walked down the hall muttering to himself, his giant shoulders hunched all the more with the weight of his quandary.

I could feel my world view begin to rattle and then crack during first semester. Dr. Brown, my writing teacher, who taught critical thinking, used a book by Bertrand Russell called *Why I Am Not A Christian.* Russell's points were provocative. His main argument was the absence of hard evidence for Jesus' divinity, resurrection, or miracles. Consequently, Jesus died for me in late October, and God was put on the critical care list in early December.

Brown was more than cynical about religion. On the last day of class, he said, "For all those who still believe in God, we've got milk and crackers for you after class." Everyone laughed, except me. Then Brown saw me. "I almost forgot, we've a minister-in-training here." I looked away.

My astronomy class added more turmoil. Professor Saunders was a believer in the Big Bang Theory. I was naive enough to ask him who was the prime mover was and he said, "Look, the scientific consensus is that the universe is a fascinating but random accident."

"What about the meaning?" I shouted. Under my desk, my palm squeezed my right fist.

"What about it Ford?"

The class tittered. I lowered my face, I was blushing.

I got a "D" in the class--my only "D" in four years. I was feeling angry with my father. He had never exposed me, or our congregation, to any alternative views. There was only warmed-over, pablum Christianity.

At least once a day I'd look at Martin's picture on my desk. My brother would know what to do. He had always located solid ground and could dance through doubt. My brother was a pathfinder, and it was now clear I wasn't.

"Ty-Ty" launched second semester by racing his moped down the hall at two in the morning. He began repeating this activity at least twice a week, usually after a drinking bout. Shaun and I would put pillows over our heads until the noise ended. We started referring to Fillmore as Fred Flintstone College.

Second semester brought one bright spot, my first class in philosophy. I was motivated, and I'd bust out and get answers. The instructor, Donald Niels, was young, had long, dirty blonde hair and big moon-shaped, brown eyes. He'd get this odd Cheshire cat smile whenever he was making a serious point. I liked him on the first day because he wore jeans and a green flannel shirt.

Early in the semester, I asked Niels for his personal philosophy. "No one really knows what's going on--it's a miracle you can walk into a restaurant, order a cup of coffee, and get something that approximates it." Then he explained that his view was called post-modernism.

Later on that day, I went to my cubicle in the library and had an imaginary talk with Niels. "Thanks, Donald--you really helped me. You explained Viet Nam. You explained why the dogs killed Martin. And you explained the cosmic two stooges, Larry and Ty-Ty. Niels, if you don't know what's going on, how the hell can I figure it out?" I added a final post script. "Niels, you've got a PhD from Princeton--is Fillmore the best you can do?"

I kept trying to get Shaun involved in my quandary. "Hey, the universe is an accident. The idea of God is a big, cosmic pacifier we're brainwashed to suck on. Life has no purpose. Doesn't that piss you off?"

Shaun would put down his book, roll his eyes and shrug. "I'm a good Catholic boy-–I don't question things." He'd pick up his book and return to studying.

One night I asked, "Doesn't it bother you that in a billion years the earth turns into a blackened cinder, the sun burns out, and our solar system collapses in on itself?"

Shaun slammed the book down on the desk. "Hell, no!" He turned his chair around to face me. "Why are you so damned intense about these things? I just live my moments. Big deal, in a billion years the show ends. It's out of our control."

"What's the purpose?"

"Shit, I don't know!"

I stopped talking to Shaun. Instead, I wrote every day in a journal. On the first page I'd write three questions in large print. What is real? What is true? What is the purpose? Every three months I would fill one up and begin another.

Outside of philosophy books, no one was talking about these questions. Reality was divided into two separate continents bisected by a massive fault line. The first reality was the alleged real world of people, houses and things; the other was a nebulous, mirage-like reality of quixotic, pulsating particles. And I had one foot on each side of these two tectonic plates. Everyday life was schizophrenic.

One Saturday night, I heard a speech from a fellow student who had similar feelings.

"Hey, fuckheads! Is anyone up there listening?"

The voice was Harry Richards, a freshman from Long Island. He was five foot six with a pumpkin-like head topped by close cut blonde hair and blue eyes. He had been a star guard on his high school basketball team but hadn't made Fillmore varsity.

"This is my last night here." He was speaking to the residents of Laher Hall from the back parking lot.

"Shut the fuck up...we're trying to sleep." A coat hanger whizzed toward Harry, who caught it and hurled it back.

"Annie broke up with me tonight...says I'm drinking too much." Harry swigged from a beer. "She's right, I am drinking too much. Shit, I don't care." He took a long gulp from his beer and tossed the can which clattered onto the pavement.

"Loser couldn't make the basketball team!" A volley of coat hangers let loose at Harry, one of which struck him in the cheek. Others pinged against his car.

"I know that's you, Erskine. I'm ready for you." Harry pulled out a switchblade. "Come on down so I can cut those tiny balls off."

Larry closed his window.

"Don't you guys get it?" Harry screamed. "You're all walking around in a dream. Everyone's asleep." He began pounding on his car hood.

"Here's a quarter, Harry--call someone who gives a shit." The quarter bounced off Harry's car.

Harry looked up at the dorm windows and yelled, "This could be *you* out here."

"Leave, then," someone yelled. Another round of coat hangers flew. One hit Harry in the cheek, drawing blood.

I looked out my window, half of the rooms had someone at the windows, but only the basketball team was responding to Harry. The rest were silent.

I wanted to yell. "Harry, you're the only one telling the truth. Keep talking. Don't leave!" but instead I went numb. "One last thing, guys." Harry turned his back, bent over, lowered his pants and mooned us. He then got into his car, honking his horn non-stop before he headed on to the highway out of town.

Sunday morning at breakfast, the news raced from table to table: seven miles out of town, Harry Richards hit a tree at ninety miles an hour. It took two hours to extricate his body. The police said it didn't look like an accident.

Later I heard laughter coming from tables where Ty-Ty, Larry, and the basketball team sat. I heard Larry imitating someone in a falsetto voice: "This could be *you* out here." Larry repeated the line to raucous laughter from his cohorts.

I was eating alone three tables away. I wanted to take my tray and smash it against his mantis face, then choke Ty-Ty. Instead, I remained motionless for a while, until I stood up, tipping my chair over and knocking my tray on the floor as I walked out. I heard Ty-Ty say to Larry, "Hey, that faggot Ford must've got his feelings hurt."

During the following week there was no official acknowledgment of any kind about what had happened. Harry had become a non-person at Millard Fillmore College. Students at school started to give directions by saying it was so many miles past Harry's tree. Shaun, my roommate, who was a biology major, said he thought the tree was dying. "No way, that tree is gonna make it."

I thought of Martin's tree and how it signaled to us that morning of its incarnation as an ice-goddess. Martin said the tree could live for another two hundred years. I promised myself I would revisit the tree, drape myself over that huge lower branch and listen for sounds of blood in her veins. Maybe all trees were interconnected. Somehow the act might keep Harry's tree alive.

All during college on the anniversary of Harry's death, I would place a single red rose by the tree.

CHAPTER 5

I spotted Thelma Sarah Menninger on the second day of freshman year. She was wearing a burgundy sweater and a grey pleated skirt. Her festive brown eyes, black hair and her flawless teeth projected a smile that could cut granite. Our eyes met, and she smiled and said "Hi" as we passed by. Her figure was provocative and I felt pulled by a subtle riptide.

I loved the colors she wore: bright greens, red, and electric blues. I learned she was an art major and I sought out her paintings which were large canvases with bold splashes of color. And I noticed that Thelma had caused a stir on campus among the males. I overheard one upper class-man: "Damn, she could stop molten lava." I winced.

Regretfully, I sensed she was out of my league. Her boyfriend went to an Ivy league college and her family were wealthy and Jewish. Plus there was this patina of New York City sophistication that she radiated.

However, she became the standard I would measure all others against. Consequently, I dated few girls during my freshman year. Later on that year, I heard she broke up with her Columbia boyfriend, but after a few months she started to date Mark Liggert, a junior and prominent jock on our campus.

Shaun McAdams got my attention in the fall of my sophomore year with some new information. "Hey, Ford, your fantasy babe is available."

"Really?" I asked.

"She and Liggert broke up. I overheard Liggert say she had a vicious temper and she's screwed up in the head."

"I bet Liggert pulled some moves. Thelma's a class act and you don't pressure her." My arms were folded in front of me.

Shaun frowned, "Be careful--there's something off with that chick."

I had to admit, there were times Thelma seemed troubled. On the days she wasn't smiling and saying hello to everyone, she'd walk across campus with her head down and her coat collar up. Her whole demeanor was pulled in, like some exotic tropical bird on a stormy day.

A few weeks later, I was going up the wide granite steps of the library and Thelma was coming down. At the halfway point, she stopped and made eye contact.

"Allen, I want to talk to you."

I was shocked. Thelma Menninger knew my name.

"Ah...um. How are you?"

"Drop the formality. I want to know when you're going to ask me out." She pushed her hair back from the side of her face and swept me with her smile. "I know I'm being forward, but I follow my intuition."

"Ah...ah...yes...I would like to go out with you."

"Good! I want you to take me to the Homecoming Dance, but beforehand we'll go out to dinner. She laughed again at my apparent bewilderment.

Then she hugged and kissed my cheek.

"Allen, you're so cute I could bite you. Well, I've got to get to my class." She walked off but turned to wave.

I felt flushed as I muttered a soft "Good-by."

I was floating a foot off the ground as I walked back to my room and reported the event to Shaun.

"No shit? She just calls you over like some peon and tells you to ask her out?"

"My fantasy woman wants me. Unbelievable!"

"You look like Cupid hit you with a ten foot harpoon."

Thelma was bold on our first date at the Green Door Restaurant, the local college hangout. We sat in a booth across from each other. "I make you nervous, don't I?" She stared into my eyes.

"Yes--you're different."

She laughed. "I've wanted to get to know you since freshman orientation." She placed her hands over my hands, which were on the table.

"I've been waiting a year for this," I said. I was blushing but I didn't care. I gripped her hands tighter.

"I know a lot about you." Thelma grinned. "First I sense you're still a virgin and I think that is wonderful!"

She admitted that she knew I was a minister's son, and that I was captain of my soccer team and vice-president of the senior class. Additionally, she mentioned that my mother was a teacher and that Gladys

Williams was my steady in high school. "And I know about your brother Martin," she added. "I'm sorry."

"How do you know so much?"

"Don't be shocked," she said. "I have my ways."

I wasn't to be outdone. "Your father is a surgeon, and you have two sisters. Your two paintings in the gallery were called 'Fall Light' and 'Nature's Rainbow.' You always wear a red scarf on Mondays."

Thelma laughed. "You've been doing homework too." She leaned over and kissed my hand. "I'm so glad we're getting to know each other."

We held hands for at least an hour. Perhaps Thelma was the reason I was at Millard Fillmore. Unlike my textbooks there was purpose and truth in those large, brown eyes, I told myself.

After dinner, we went to the dance. We did all the slow dances draped over each other. I walked her home to Abigail Adams Dormitory. We found a darkened corner and made out against a large white column. I could barely walk back to my dorm sporting what might have been the largest erection in the history of Millard Fillmore College. My last few reservations about the morality of premarital sex were gone.

We had three glorious weeks before I met Thelma's dark side. Her shadow surfaced as we were sitting in our favorite booth at the Green Door. I'd just gotten the bill. "Thelma, I'm two dollars short. Can you help out?"

Before she could exhale, her face turned Medusa-like.

"I don't believe you're doing this!" she snapped. She slammed herself back into the booth, arms folded, her radiant smile now a mocking sneer. She stood up, grabbed her coat, and threw her water on me, then slammed the door as she left the restaurant. Everyone saw the show. Dumbstruck and water logged I remained frozen.

Three days later, there was a tentative knock on my door. Thelma was there looking like a lost first grader.

"I'm sorry, I over-reacted. Please forgive me." She offered me a tentative smile and those big brown, pleading eyes. She kissed me and whispered, "Everything will be okay now."

My resistance collapsed under the onslaught. Peace reigned until the next outburst a month later, when I was fifteen minutes late for a date. Again we made up, but the pattern became familiar. A perceived slight, followed by a verbal bashing and a tossing of water--depending of course on availability. This would be followed, several days later, by an apology and her favorite mantra: "Everything will be okay."

When I brought Thelma home that Thanksgiving she made an impact on my mother and father. Everyone was taken with her charm, looks, and intelligence.

"She's so bright and so talented," my mother said in an aside to me in the kitchen.

Uncle Herbie leaned over to me during the dinner. "She's quite a catch."

I smiled. I was certain that God had sent Thelma to me.

Thanksgiving Day dinner went well until dessert. "Okay, who wants pumpkin pie?" Mom always pretended that no one liked her pumpkin pie.

A chorus of 'I do's' went up from around the table.

Thelma was silent.

"What about you, Thelma?" my mother asked.

"*I hate pumpkin pie!*" said Thelma.

The table went silent. My mother looked startled, and my stomach dropped to the floor.

Thelma mumbled something about an allergy to pumpkins and tried to start a conversation about Picasso's *Guernica.* Uncle Herbie pitched in, but he knew nothing about art. The rest of dessert was eaten with little conversation.

Later that night my father was in his study polishing one of his antique oil cans from his oddball collection. "There's something peculiar about that girl," he said to me.

"Dad, she's working on her problems." I surprised myself by how confident I sounded. "Don't judge her by only one incident."

My father looked at me funny and went back to polishing the can.

That night before I went to sleep, I thought about Martin and when he'd started high school, and how girls began to drop by the house. I was usually irritated by them and would walk away when they arrived.

"Bro," he told me, "girls are cool, but the thing is to stay relaxed around them."

I was either tense or excited around Thelma.

CHAPTER 6

Even with Thelma in my life, Shaun still thought I was too intense about everything. "Ford, lighten up—you're like a cat chasing its tail."

"I'm intellectually constipated," I said. "I'm not an unquestioning, good-natured Catholic drone like you."

"Spend more time with Thelma—that girl exudes Ex-lax."

I threw my pillow at Shaun. I envied him. Problems would push him down briefly, but he would always bob back up like a cork.

In my agitation about purpose and the nature of things, one thought kept recurring. Mom knew a lot and seemed sure of herself. I decided to go home and seek her help. Dad was away at a conference. She met me at the bus station in New Haven and drove me home.

"Your color looks off," she said. "What's wrong? Thelma?"

"No."

"What is it?"

"I don't know. Everything."

"Allen, be specific."

"I don't know. Jesus. God. Religion. I'm doubting everything."

My mother pointed to the now cleared mahogany dining room table, and we sat down—at opposite ends. She got out her ashtray, Marlboros, and poured herself a second glass of wine.

I studied her in a new way. She was now forty-seven, still a classy dresser—and always well groomed. Her face had perfect symmetry: cheekbones, forehead, chin, brown eyes and brunette hair pulled back in a bun. She had no close friends. The only time I saw her cry was at Martin's funeral.

"I gave up my questions a long time ago," she said. "They're all circular." She laughed and then put her hand over her mouth.

"Mom--what is it?"

"Perhaps you should know my big secret--you're of age now."

"What?"

She sat up in her chair. "No one knows this but I've been an agnostic since college."

"Does Dad know?"

"Not a clue!" She took another sip from her wine and gave me a rare smile. "And you're never to repeat this confidence to anyone."

I nodded and swallowed. "How can you stay married?"

"I've become a seasonal actress over the years." She exhaled again. "Allen, there's no wizard–we're all alone.

I was trembling. "What's the point then?"

"We are part of a life cycle. We're born, we mature and we die."

"But...?"

My mother saw my look of disappointment. "Allen, you're too sensitive about everything."

She exhaled smoke out of both nostrils and for a moment she reminded me of a dragon.

"Don't you hope for something?" I could feel myself gripping the table's edges with both hands.

"Once in a while," she said, and she got a faraway look, then grimaced. "Martin's death was the *coup-de-gras.* A youth with his promise killed in such an obscene manner is the ultimate abomination." She blew a stream of smoke straight up in the air. "After Martin's death I shifted again. Technically I'm an atheist." She took another long sip from her wine. "It feels wonderful to say that--in a parsonage of all places." I sipped from my now warm Coke and watched my mother's smoke drift upward like incense.

I became aware of a small red spot inside of me growing bigger and hotter by the moment. I wanted to overturn the table. *"Is that the best you can do? Your beliefs are shit!"* I swallowed my epithet.

I removed my sweating hands from the table's edge and excused myself, and went upstairs to my room. I locked the door and fell face down on my bed, and began pounding my mattress as I released a riptide of deep sobs. I hadn't cried in seven years.

Later I rolled over and faced the ceiling. 'Maybe I'd set Martin up. "Maybe part of me wanted him to die...I wasn't sure...maybe if I'd charged in with the Bowie knife we could've killed all the dogs. On the other hand maybe I was a clever Cain, not even I knew I'd killed my brother. I rolled back on my face and let more waves of crying flow. Exhausted, I fell off to sleep.

Later that night I went to the bathroom and noticed a light coming from my mother's study at the end of the hall. I peered in. She was working on an oil portrait of Martin. She had started it three years ago, and would work on it off and on. Now she was putting shadows in Martin's green sweater.

"Sometimes I think you never want to finish that painting."

She jumped at the sound of my voice and after glancing at me returned to her steady, sure brush strokes. "This painting," she said, "is both my remembrance and my penance."

I closed the door muttering, "She spends more time painting her dead son than she does listening to her living one."

"I heard that," she said and she came out to the hall. "Martin was head and shoulders above all of us. He was gifted in ways none of us could ever hope for."

I glared at her.

"By the way, I never asked you to explain the Bowie knife you had on your belt that day you ran into the living room."

I turned around and walked to my room. I got up the next morning at six, grabbed my bag, and hitchhiked to New Haven. Several weeks later my mother sent a perfunctory apology letter, but I didn't communicate with her or my father for three months.

One of the habits I picked up from my high school teachers was to read the *New York Times* as a conscious act of self-education. In April of 1970, I flipped through most of the sections until I came to the book review section. The cover story hailed a new book entitled *Street Gang Leaders* which was written by a twenty-eight year old sociologist by the name of Sydney Hammond, III. He had worked with the gangs as a social worker.

The reviewer said Hammond's work was the finest piece of social science writing in the last thirty years and was destined for national recognition. I took an immediate dislike to the smug, freckled face of Hammond that was on the front page.

Nonetheless, something compelled me to read the story. The young sociologist had studied ten street gang leaders in Los Angeles. The reviewer said Hammond's description of a particular charismatic gang leader known as Rasputin was brilliant:

> Never had I observed a youth so brimming with his promise. Perhaps one in a hundred thousand have the constellation of genes

> that structure such an uncommon intelligence, appearance and personality.
>
> I was amazed how the gravitational pull of his personality kept dozens of gang members in continuous orbit about him. Yet, despite the gifts something was missing. One sensed, inside, a feverish radar screen sweeping twenty four hours a day. Despite all his acolytes Rasputin has no real brother.

Hammond concluded by saying, "Environment always trumps genes in the history of gang leaders." He said the dangers of drugs, violence, and other variables gave gang leaders short life spans. In fact, Rasputin disappeared one year later without a trace. "No doubt dead from a drug overdose or murdered by a rival gang."

Near the end of the article I could feel something unusual happening to me. There was a surge going through my body. Rasputin wasn't dead--instinctively I knew he was alive. Another awareness hit: somehow, even in this moment I was connected to him. The thing was crazy but it felt like a kind of remembrance. I told Thelma about the article and my feeling of a connection.

"That's absurd!" she said. "You're a minister's son and he's a gang leader--what could you two have in common?" She sighed and clicked her tongue.

Later that day I told Shaun about Rasputin, and how I felt drawn to him. He rolled his eyes at me and went back to his book. I clipped the article and put it inside one of my favorite books, *East of Eden* by Steinbeck.

I then ordered Hammond's book and read it on the day I received it. Rasputin got his name, I learned, when he was setup by five rival gang leaders who were trying to kill him. During the fight he was stabbed a number of times. At the end of the fight two opponents held him down, while a third used a knife to carve a large X on his back. The mark was a sign of humiliation.

He was hospitalized for one month and made a rapid recovery. His nickname came from the gang members who watched the fight and saw him return from the dead like the Russian monk who couldn't be killed.

A year later Rasputin was controlling twelve different gangs in East Los Angeles. He operated from a large warehouse which was a fence for the stereos, TV's and car radios which were the gang's specialty. He was secretive about his identity and always wore a Lone Ranger type mask at gang meetings. He was six two, jet black hair, wide shoulders and a narrow waist.

Hammond noted a change at his final meeting, the one before he disappeared; Hammond noted a change. Rasputin was speaking to over one hundred gang members at their warehouse. He told the members what they were doing had to change. Afterwards, Hammond interviewed one of his lieutenants who said Rasputin got a vision from a dream about how things would change in the future. However, Rasputin disappeared a week later and no one ever saw him again.

After a few months, my fantasies about finding Rasputin faded. However, I held on to Hammond's book and would skim it occasionally. Although I still felt I was supposed to connect with him, I was baffled at how this was supposed to occur.

"Hey, Ford, can I sit with you?" I heard.

I looked up and saw Ivan Campbell, a tall, geeky, bearded junior who was well known on campus as an eccentric Einstein with an A average. He had flunked out of M.I.T.--or been thrown out, no one was sure.

"Okay," I said.

Campbell sat across from me, his breakfast tray covered with two small boxes of Cheerios, five pieces of toast, four bananas, and a book by Wittgenstein.

"I was in that astronomy class when Saunders put you down," he said. "Your question, although naive, was the most genuine thing that happened in that class. Saunders is an asshole." He peeled back all his bananas, one by one, and decapitated them two at a time. He then stated that philosophically, there was little we could really know; he was a skeptic. I winced at his response.

Then he delivered a scathing critique of Millard Fillmore's faculty, administration, and student body. "I realize now that I came here because I wanted to do field research on an obscure, primitive sub-culture," he laughed. "I've already filled up two notebooks with the antics of the basketball team."

He emitted a shrill laugh and told me to come by his room later. I dropped by that night. His room was a mess. One entire side had car parts strewn about. He was rebuilding a 1952 Studebaker. At least seven books were spread across his desk. They, in turn, were covered with piles of note cards with strange symbols on them.

"I'm teaching myself Mandarin Chinese. I believe in about twenty years it will have great value."

In another corner of the desk was a half-opened box of Saltine crackers and a six pack of Pepsi. His clothes were scattered everywhere. A huge, four foot high brass water pipe sat in the center of the room, next to some pillows.

"Hey, you're just in time, Ford." He stood up and grabbed several packages wrapped with Christmas paper. He started ripping them open.

"What gives? This is March."

He held up a green tartan flannel shirt against his chest. "Looks good, huh?"

I nodded.

"I wait till March to open my Christmas presents. I hate the way the primitives here wear new clothes right after Christmas."

We talked that night for hours. Ivan understood my search. His weird laugh continued to punctuate his comments. We ended the evening by agreeing to form a coterie of seekers.

There were, however, some disturbing differences between Ivan and me. He said Saunders had been rude but truthful: there was no purpose in the design of the universe. I told Ivan that I sensed, somehow, a purpose–and he sneered and laughed. He said he'd read everything significant on the topic of cosmology and that skepticism was the only rational option.

When I left his room I felt depressed. Ivan was an egocentric, smug bastard but I was desperate for allies in my four year sentence at M.F.C. Although he could never be a brother, we could be partners out of necessity. Somehow, we were going to make a difference. After several meetings, we decided to call our group the Philosopher's Club. We debated possible members and interviewed a half dozen students. Only one student accepted our invitation. René Pritchard was a bright and inquisitive freshman who had red hair and looked like Alfred E. Neumann. He was excited by our invitation but seemed intimidated by the fact we were upperclassmen. We held our first meeting a week later and discussed objectives.

"Let's burn down the R.O.T.C. building." Ivan was puffing on his huge, brass water pipe. I watched the large glass container bubble and gurgle--madly--as though it were a hologram of Ivan's brain at work.

"How much pot is in that thing?" I asked. "There is no R.O.T.C. program here."

"My God, you're right. I must have been thinking of M.I.T. Isn't there something we could burn?"

"The campus is all brick buildings," René said.

"I've got it!" Ivan put down the stem of the water pipe and slapped his thigh. "We can set fire to ourselves like the Buddhist monks did in Vietnam. Imagine that: Millard Fillmore's brightest intellects protest mediocrity and meaninglessness. The papers and media would give it a lot of play."

René had dropped his Pepsi and was choking. I whacked him hard on the back.

"Ivan, for Christ sake, we wouldn't be around to appreciate our good deed," I said. I wasn't sure if he was playing with us.

"You're kidding, right?" René looked at both of us for reassurance. "My parents are liberal, but they would never go that far."

After a number of meetings we found a vehicle we all agreed on. We decided to publish an underground newspaper as a way to express our frustrations. We liked the concept and began brainstorming ideas.

We named our paper the *Popsicle Stick.* Our college President, Taylor Tyler, had a fondness for the delicacy and was frequently seen licking and slurping his way around campus in all seasons. We agreed the name would symbolize Millard Fillmore College's penchant for the mundane.

The first issue of the *Popsicle Stick* featured an in-depth evaluation of all of the professors including letter grades, anecdotal comments, and a critical review of their teaching effectiveness. A majority of faculty received C's, a few got D's. We made sure every professor received copies.

The students loved the paper. The faculty and administration were livid. We heard that President Tyler was especially miffed because of our name.

"Hey, let's make the next issue about Buzz Frick." René was smiling as he recalled Frick, our campus cop, standing outside his room sniffing for marijuana.

One month later, the *Popsicle Stick's* lead story was entitled, "The Most Incompetent Campus Cop in America." Frick was in his sixties, overweight and not too bright. Last spring, late one night, he had fired shots in the air near Abigail Adams dorm. Buzz thought he saw a man entering through a second story window in the girl's dorm. Afterward, Dean of Students, Halloran, had confirmed that no intruder had been found. However Frick was never reprimanded.

René did some research and confirmed that Frick was a first cousin of Ann Tyler, President Tyler's wife. The story focused on the shooting and reports of other incompetencies. News reached us that Frick was running all over campus trying to confiscate copies.

Ivan stumbled into my room doubled-up with laughter. "Ford, I don't believe it! Frick was going from table to table inside the library ripping copies out of student's hands. The librarian tried to stop him and they got into a shouting match."

The Philosopher's Club became more emboldened. I proposed that it was time to publicize Millard Fillmore's worst secret--Abner Townsend's dalliance with his sheep. René and Ivan encouraged me. After three weeks of sleuthing, I found a copy of the 1871 trial of Abner Townsend.

Our college's benefactor was indeed caught, red-handed, having carnal knowledge of one of his sheep. The cross-species tryst had been interrupted by the local Presbyterian minister, who reported it to the authorities.

The headline for the next paper read, "Torrid Tales of Townsend." The article was devoted to a summary of the trial, and a history of the cover-ups by the local historical society and the college. I got up at four in the morning and dropped off piles of the issue all over the campus.

All of our papers were gone by noon. The reaction of the students and faculty was positive. Dr. Jameson cited the article in his American History class as a quality example of primary source utilization.

We needed another story to top the Abner expose. We decided to take the ultimate risk: our group would take on the basketball team. One month later, our fourth issue came out, "Halitosis, Hangers and Honor" was the headline. I wrote the feature story focusing on the antics of Larry and Ty-Ty. René did a story verifying how Ty-Ty got his grade illegally changed from an F to a D in Biology. Ivan did background research confirming that the team was cited eight times for mooning people from the bus during their away games. I was nervous this time; the basketball team would be furious and Ty-Ty had an awful temper.

Additionally, I wrote a tongue-in-cheek editorial that proposed a radical solution for the basketball team.

> Darwin studied life in the Galapagos Islands because evolution occurred there in unique ways, which is why we suggest the basketball team be exiled there.
>
> Their mission will be to breed with the island's indigenous creatures thereby creating an exciting acceleration of biological aberrations. We also suggest, that President Tyler initiate an early retirement and become the first game warden.
>
> We also recommend that the college alumni erect a large statue of Abner Townsend there since he was a pioneer in cross species mating.

By ten in the morning, a majority of students had a copy of the paper. Even Frick was sitting on a park bench reading a copy and pulling on his chin.

At noon I saw Larry and Ty-Ty in the quadrangle surrounded by members of the team. Ty-Ty's face was contorted and he was thrashing the air with both arms. "I'm gonna kill the bastards! I'm gonna kill 'em!"

I walked past the team with my head down, trying not to smile. Larry was trying to soothe Ty-Ty. "We'll find 'em, and fix 'em good."

Thelma was suspicious about my possible involvement in the paper. "You know something," she said, "and you won't tell me." I'd smile a bit and plead ignorance. If she pressed me more, I'd blow her kisses and whisper endearments. Still, she commented that I seemed happier, more relaxed.

CHAPTER 7

During my breaks and vacations home I tried avoiding my father whenever possible. When we did connect I started to bait him–especially at dinnertime.

"Dad, at the Sermon on the Mount, couldn't the crowd have hidden the loaves of bread and wine under their robes?"

"We have to accept the literal biblical version of those events." My father frowned.

"But the information is all second or third hand. There is no way to know if any of the miracles ever happened."

"Look, the bottom line is that Christianity is based on a leap of faith. There's little hard proof." My dad had stopped eating.

"How can people build their lives on hearsay?"

"The majority of people get there!" My father hit the table with his palm. "Is this what college has done for you--turned you into the resident Doubting Thomas?" He left the table.

My mother smiled, caught herself and told me not to push my father so hard. The rest of spring break was spent in awkward dinnertime silences.

On the second day home, on my summer break, my father grabbed me. "Allen, we've got to talk." Dad was using his minister's voice and he ushered me to his study, pulling the pocket doors closed behind him. It was only my second day home, for the summer.

"What's going on?" he asked. "I feel this growing wall of ice between us," he said.

I swallowed, telling myself I couldn't really confront him. "I've lost respect for you," I said.

Dad spilled his coffee. "Why?"

"I know about the affair with Louise Fredrich and I've watched you skim money from the collection plate." I hesitated but spat out the words: "I feel set-up by you!"

"Over what?"

"You shut out contrary ideas. You have no original thoughts. All you offer is warmed-over Christianity." My voice was breaking. "Right now I'm fighting like hell to stay afloat."

"Why didn't you tell me?"

"You can't hear doubts!"

"That isn't true!"

"Wake up! Christianity is based on a half-baked story that a virgin laid down on the ground, spread her legs and a divine seed blew into her. Eureka! A son is born who then dies on a cross. Presto! He comes back to life. Presto again! He's the Son of God. Hallelujah! The masses are saved and the planet transformed. The story is bullshit!"

"You're distorting everything, Allen."

My jaw felt tight and my voice deepened: "I feel sorry for Bob Ford--he's a two-penny huckster for this crap."

Dad's tone became mocking. "So in a few year's study at college, you divined that two thousand years of Christian tradition was at best a children's story?"

"Yes, that's about it," I said. I didn't blink.

"Now, you're going to turn your back on your heritage and run from it?"

My left leg was trembling, and my mind was racing. I could find no response.

"Isn't that what you did to Martin? Turned your back and ran?"

I felt slammed against the wall by the comment. "Dad, that isn't true! I was twelve years old. I was running to get help."

"You abandoned your brother!" Dad shouted: "You let him down! Now you're doing it to me."

"That's bullshit!" I yelled. "There wasn't anything I could do! He was two hundred feet away...the dogs were huge...everything happened too fast!"

"You could've grabbed something and gone in there. There were two of you." Dad put his hands on his hips. "Your mother told me about the Bowie knife. You were big enough, you could have killed a dog or two. *Martin didn't have to die!"* he screamed.

"Yeah, I could've gone in there. Today you would've had two dead sons."

Dad's face twisted. "Martin didn't have to die."

New anger was rising and I regained my voice. "What about *your God*? Martin screamed for Him. *Where was He?"*

"You let your brother down." Dad was now crying and shaking.

"What you do is far worse. You teach fable as fact. Your vocation kills the truth!"

"Get out of this house! Get out!"

I picked up the huge, gilt edged family Bible that was Dad's favorite possession. "I hate this book! I hate you!" I heaved the book at dad's collection of oil cans, which flew, clattering in a dozen directions. "And I hate Martin!"

I stormed out of the house yelling, "Nietzsche is right--God is dead!" I ran to Ollie Stevenson's house and threw open the screen door and walked into their living room where they were all sitting on the sofa watching the Red Sox. I stood in front of their TV set.

"Jee-Jee-sus, what's wrong?" Ollie asked. Mr. and Mrs. Stevenson crossed their arms and stared at me.

"I've had it with my asshole father!" I said. Then I told the Stevensons about our fight. I told them that I'd called him a huckster for the all-American superstition of Christianity. "Do you believe it? He blames me for Martin's death?" I had to catch my breath. "Can I stay here?"

Mr. and Mrs. Stevenson agreed that I could stay for awhile. I did insist, though, that they take down the crucifix that was on the wall in their guest room. I could tell I made Ollie's parents nervous with my new found atheism.

Word got around in Greenfield about the fallout between Reverend Bob and the number two son. Wherever I went, I broadcast the story to anyone who listened. I hoped Gladys Williams would hear of my emergence as an avowed atheist. And I fantasized being a guest speaker at the Pilgrim Fellowship. I'd pass out pictures of Nietzche and read from Bertrand Russell's book. I even went out of my way to tell Sam Walters, Chair of the Board of Deacons, what had happened.

The letter of apology came in early July, one month after the blowup. Dad said it was unfair to have blamed me for Martin's death. He asked me to move back. Mom brokered the details of our cease-fire. First, we agreed to not discuss religion. Second, we agreed not to discuss Martin's death. I moved back a week later.

During the first week home the house felt enshrouded by a dense cloud of tension. First, Dad and I looked the other way as we walked by each other, and at the dinner table, we continued to avoid eye contact, usually talking through Mom. We made a few cursory attempts at discussing the Red Sox, but it was forced. Mom said Dad was angry about how I'd fanned the blow-out throughout Greenfield. Parishioners were still talking. Our fragile peace reminded me of the Cold War between Russia and America. Both of us knew we each had powerful weapons that could devastate the other; however, the awareness created a perverse kind of equilibrium.

I looked forward to returning to my junior year at college. Thelma and I would have more time and the Philosophers' Club could strike again in some new venue.

CHAPTER 8

The second year of the Philosophers' Club got off to an erratic start. We put out three more editions of the *Popsicle Stick*, but we had few sensational stories and I noticed untouched stacks all over campus. Also, Ivan and I were arguing more about our direction as well as our personal beliefs. René sometimes left our meetings early, shaking his head. However, in late fall, we came up with a winner. We decided to seize the symbol of our college's academic life: Townsend Tower. Our takeover would make the ultimate political statement.

Our group put four months of planning into the mission. Ivan stole a master key from one of the janitors and we sneaked into the tower on three different occasions to scope out the facility and review details. We were all anxious as we navigated our way up the endless flights of worn, dusty stairs, trying to avoid the layers of dried pigeon shit and canopies of cobwebs. I even stuck my head out on the small balcony where I'd make my speech. On our last foray, we installed four large dead bolts inside the thick oak entrance door.

"Officer Frick will have to huff and puff to get this door down," said René. We all laughed at the picture of our overweight, aging campus constable straining both mentally and physically to deal with the door. We hugged as a group while Ivan recited an ancient Chinese war prayer in his best Mandarin accent.

The seizure of the tower was scheduled for the second Thursday in May. Perversely, we rejoiced when we found out it was President Tyler's sixtieth birthday.

On the night before the seizure, René stole a bullhorn from the physical education department. We met in Ivan's room at ten the next morning and started taking turns smoking from the pot-filled water pipe and drinking from our twelve-pack of Colt 45 beer that Ivan had bought. Just before noon Ivan removed the stem of his water pipe from his mouth. "This is a historic day in Millard Fillmore history." He closed his eyes for a few moments and then said he would write about my action in his autobiography. He did his strange laugh for an extra ten seconds.

"Assuming Frick shoots me, your write-up may be my only chance at the history books." I was feeling loose from the beers.

René sipped from his beer and smiled at me. "What a way to end your junior year!"

The time was now one fifty in the afternoon. I packed my gym bag with the bullhorn and another can of beer. Ivan had finished writing the placards listing our ninety-two demands in both English and Mandarin Chinese. His task was to nail the poster board signs, beforehand to the main entrance doors of Townsend Tower. I dressed in my cleanest chinos and a pink oxford cloth button-down shirt. I even polished my brown loafers. My appearance would be a class act.

I checked myself in the mirror--Thelma would want me to look spiffy, although she had no idea of our plans. Ivan made me promise--from the outset--not to tell Thelma. "Your girlfriend is one unguided missile," as he shook his head.

I grabbed my gym bag and headed for the building. I nodded and smiled to students as I made my way to the site.

I opened the door to the clock tower at one fifty-five. I was careful to slide the four bolts to lock the door from the inside. I walked slowly up the creaking stairs and appeared on the balcony at one fifty-nine. I stood under the clock in the cramped balcony. One hundred and forty feet up, no one noticed me. Soon I'd be playing the role of a young Socrates, or was I a young Martin Luther? I was feeling muddled.

At two o'clock Ivan pulled the fire alarm. Hundreds of agitated students and their professors began pouring out of their classrooms spilling into the quadrangle below. Next, René shot off the flare. The smoke and light caught everyone's attention as it exploded over the tower.

Elation filled me. Millard Fillmore College's students would finally wake up. I spoke into the bullhorn, holding it in my left hand and sipping my beer with the other. The flare had reached its zenith.

"Good afternoon fellow students. Townsend Hall has been seized and classes canceled."

The seven hundred or so students in the quadrangle below cheered. "Welcome to the new market place of ideas." The students had quieted and were listening.

"Hey, asshole, I'm paying money to hear my professor--not you!" I ignored the comment.

"Hear me out," I said. I began to sweat.

Larry Erskine had his hands cupped over his mouth. "Hey Ford, why don't you jump?"

"Hey, Erskine, you're one of the reasons I'm up here! You're a hero because you throw a piece of inflated animal skin through a metal hoop. Big deal! Why don't you and your Neanderthal friends take your coat hangers and look for a mastodon."

I took another long sip of my beer. Larry shook his fist at me. "I'll get you for this." He and his colony stomped out of the quadrangle.

"By the way, why was the basketball team never disciplined for their actions at Laher Hall?"

It was then that I noticed President Taylor Tyler and Dean of Students Halloran entering the quadrangle. Frick was trudging along behind them. Tyler had a bullhorn in his hands. He marched directly to the center of the quadrangle and put the bullhorn to his mouth.

"Ford, I know that's you up there. You're breaking a host of rules--come down this instant!"

"No! I'm exercising my first amendment privilege."

Sirens whirled and two police cars and the fire department's ancient ladder truck pulled into the quadrangle. The police and firemen ran over to President Tyler and formed in a huddle. Then Tyler aimed the bullhorn at me.

"Ford, this is the last time I'll ask you to come down. You're out of order."

"No! President Tyler. You're out of order! This whole campus is out of order! This seizure is an attempt to restore order and meaning to this campus."

"You're jeopardizing your college career." Tyler had decided to extend our symposium.

"No. I'm restoring it. This take-over is the best thing I've ever done in my life!" All of the students were quiet. No one was leaving.

"What's your point, Ford?"

"Besides being mediocre, this college gives us no sense of purpose."

"Prove it."

"C'mon, how many students really feel confused, or unsure in their lives? C'mon, don't be afraid."

One by one, hands went up until more than half of the students had supported my cause.

"For Chrissake, President Tyler, turn around and look at those hands! They're telling you something!"

Tyler glanced over his shoulder, looked at the students, and turned back.

"You're manipulating their emotions by your theatrics. This is not a scientific poll?"

"Tyler, don't you see? Millard Fillmore College doesn't work. We want more."

As if planned, the students began a low chant which quickly grew louder, *"We want more! We want more! We want more!"*

Dean Halloran ran up to President Tyler and whispered to him. Tyler smiled and raised the bullhorn to his lips. "Your parents were called and will be here in a few hours. Your father is very upset."

"Go, Ford! Go, Ford!" The students were chanting again.

"The firemen are going to take you down with the ladder," Tyler said. He then yelled to the fireman, "Get him down--fast."

"Notice how nervous the administration gets when a student speaks his mind." I took one last long draft from the beer can and tossed it in Tyler's direction.

"We want more! We want more!"

"I've questions for you, President Tyler. Why do the maintenance men find so many liquor bottles in your rubbish can on Monday morning? Are you confused? Are you in pain? Are you?"

"No! You're repeating a nasty rumor."

"Why do we get one point of view here? Dr. Niels, c'mon, what do you believe--deep in your heart? And don't say you believe only in free inquiry--it's too easy."

Niels folded his arms and frowned.

The firemen's ladders were fully extended--ten feet short of the balcony.

"Go, Ford! Go, Ford!"

"Why is our college named after the most mediocre President in history?" I said. "Why can't we change the name?"

A student's voice rose from the quadrangle. "Abner Townsend College would make more sense." Everyone laughed.

"And another thing," I said. "Why did the Harry Richards' affair get so hushed up? A student kills himself and he becomes a non-person. Why?."

Buzz Frick was now making his way through the crowd, pulling Thelma by the hand. He gave her the bullhorn with Tyler's approval.

"Allen, what are you doing up there? You'll get expelled. What about us? What about me?" Thelma began to cry then shouted, "You come down here this instant!"

"Thelma, they're using you," I said.

"Go, Thelma! Go, Thelma!"

Thelma pivoted towards the students and bellowed into the bullhorn, "Shut up, assholes! This is between Allen and me." The students quieted, and she turned around towards me.

"I left a letter for you at your dorm," I said. "Read it--don't let them manipulate you. Please."

"Allen, I love you."

"I love you, too, Thelma."

The students cheered.

President Tyler grabbed the bullhorn back from Thelma.

I became aware of the sound of splintering wood as the firemen's axes chopped through the bolted entrance door.

"They're coming for me. All I've done is ask questions. They're afraid...they're about to silence me. Tell them again what you want."

"We want more! We want more!"

Just then, Frick, covered in sweat, red-faced, veins bulging in his forehead, broke out onto the balcony with his gun drawn. I raised my hands over my head and he put handcuffs on me.

"Go Ford! Go Ford! Go Ford!"

Upon seeing me led off the balcony President Tyler picked up his bullhorn. "Okay, folks, the show is over. You're all expected to return to class."

The crowd meekly dispersed, but I heard a loud voice yell, "Abner Townsend fucked sheep." I smiled as I was escorted to President Tyler's office. I'd done something. Once inside the administration building, I was brought to Tyler's office and told to sit in a plush red leather chair opposite his desk. I was still smiling and giddy from the beers. Two police officers stayed in the outer office. The first sight to greet me in the President's office was a huge portrait of a smiling Abner Townsend looking down at me from behind President Tyler's desk, and I wondered if the look was because Abner had just finished frolicking with one of his cloven footed femme fatales.

Buzz Frick entered the room and undid my handcuffs.

"You're in big trouble. The oak door will cost you a lot of money," he said.

"Frick, did you hear what I said?"

"That stuff was communist agitation. President Nixon's been warning us. I seen it on TV."

My parents showed up later. Dad was furious and Mom distant. President Tyler and Dean Halloran took them to an adjoining conference room. They offered my parents a proposal: they would drop legal charges if I would go to a psychiatric hospital for observation. Dean Halloran had found an opening for me in a facility in Albany, and my parents agreed.

During the time I was being held, I could hear Thelma in an outside office making demands, crying or shouting. Buzz Frick came in during the first hour. The front of his shirt was soaked. "Jesus, what's wrong with that girlfriend of yours? She just threw a glass of water on me."

Thelma was brought in just before I was to leave with my parents. "I knew this would happen! They're putting you away!" She repeatedly hugged and kissed me. "When will I ever see you again? This is terrible!" My mother took her into another room to calm her.

I looked out the window and saw a state police car and several more town police cars. I noticed several reporters taking pictures and talking to people. I was beginning to doubt the wisdom of my actions.

The car ride to the Albany psychiatric hospital seemed to take forever. Dad ranted for a full hour. "I can't believe you did this. You could lose your scholarship. Besides, no one wants a minister who's a flaky radical. This is because of Martin, isn't it?"

Mom said nothing, eyes straight ahead.

"Dad, if you were Jesus now, what would you be saying?"

My father swore under his breath; my mother elbowed him hard; he said nothing on the last hour of the trip. We arrived late that night and were processed at the main desk. My father stayed in the car.

On my first full day, I met with a young psychologist, Dr. Tom Wilde. He asked a few general questions, then let me talk. He smiled often and even laughed when I told him about the Philosophers' Club, Thelma, my search, and the seizure of Townsend Tower. His eyes widened when I told him about Martin and the dogs.

At the end of our second counseling session, he gave me his assessment. "I don't think there's anything seriously wrong with you. The fancy name for your condition is an identity crisis." Dr. Wilde added that in most ways, I was normal. However, he added, seizing an academic building while intoxicated, was extreme. "I'm going to recommend you be released after a week's observation."

I was elated. I sauntered back to my room, lay on the bed with my hands behind my head. "So, communist agitators are normal!" I laughed and fell asleep.

The next morning, I saw Dr. Wilde again. He was frowning. "We've got a problem. My superior, Dr. Mirar, is a conservative psychiatrist. He was upset when he heard my recommendations."

Wilde then told me that Dean Halloran had talked to Mirar and painted a picture of an out-of-control student who had plunged the college into mayhem–and that Dr. Mirar felt I should be there a minimum of six weeks.

"So what do we do?" I asked.

"Mirar wants to see you this afternoon. The key is not to lose your temper. He'll be testing you."

"Thanks."

Dr. Alfred Mirar was a small, balding, pudgy man with a goatee. "Well, young Ford, you stirred up things quite a bit at your college."

"Yes, I did. And I'm glad."

"Do you have a drinking problem?"

"No."

"Are you suicidal?"

"No."

"Do you have any thoughts about killing anyone?"

"No. Although my government is interested in providing me with vocational training opportunities in Vietnam."

"Amusing." Mirar gave me a wry smile.

Wilde and Mirar reached a compromise. I would be kept at the hospital for a two week observation period. If there was nothing unusual, I'd be sent home.

I kept one lie going throughout my internment. I said I acted alone; I wanted to protect René and Ivan. I was pleased when I received a letter from Ivan in my second week. He explained that he'd begun nailing our ninety-two demands on the doors only to be stricken by a case of severe diarrhea. He spent the next hour in the basement men's room of Townsend Tower. René, he said, panicked when he saw the police cars, threw our leaflets behind a bush and ran back to the dorm.

Thelma wrote some kind of letter to me every day. She either called me brave or foolish. The letters irritated and entertained me. I saved all of them, which pleased Thelma.

On my last day there, Mirar and Wilde held an exit interview. They both said I was too intense and needed to lighten up. I wondered if they had talked to Shaun McAdams.

My mother came and drove me home. She said my hospital stay had strained my parents' relationship, and my father was now taking tranquilizers. I smiled. "I guess it's part of the life cycle, Mom."

It had been nine years since Martin's death and I mused about the status of my friendships on the way home. Ollie kept in touch but he wasn't haunted by my cosmic questions. I felt affection for Shaun and liked his sunny optimism, but his world view was too simplistic for me. And I felt let down by both René and Ivan; they had choked at the critical hour.

Added to this was a recurring dream where I would find Rasputin by Martin's tree but he would walk away from me and disappear in the woods.

"Face it Ford," I told myself. "You have absolutely no close male friend."

CHAPTER 9

Days after I left the Albany Psychiatric Hospital I met Thelma's favorite relatives, Uncle Harold and Aunt Marion whom she had been living with since her parents retired to Miami. She was eager to have me meet them. "I can't believe how they spoil me," she laughed, and pointed to her expensive gold Elgin watch.

The couple lived in a brownstone in Brooklyn Heights. A tall man in his late fifties with a pleasant face and a pear shaped body answered the door. He ushered us into a spacious, book-lined parlor. He hugged Thelma a number of times and said, "my little boychika."

Then Aunt Marion fussed over Thelma, telling her she looked too thin. Thelma beamed in their presence.

I stood back. Earlier, Thelma had told me she and her uncle had argued about the fact she was dating a "goy."

After the amenities, I turned to Harold. "Now Dr. Menninger, I'm curious about your academic interests. I've been on a bit of a quest." I knew he was a Professor of Religious Studies at Yeshiva University.

"Well, well." He arched his eyebrow. "Yes, yes, I do love to discuss these things." He laughed and pointed to a grouping of chairs, where we sat as he explained that his academic specialty was studying mysticism from a cross-cultural perspective. Thelma was frowning, irritated that attention in the room had shifted from her.

"How does mysticism help the person in the street?" I asked Harold.

"Ah, a good, practical question." Then he said our modern, rationalistic culture had stripped away references to the transcendent. He believed there was a great body of evidence to support something astounding at the heart of human experience. "Some people called it oneness, union, or all-embracing love." He said the phenomenon was the touchstone of every religion.

I shared with him a shortened version of my three years of wandering in the philosophical desert of Millard Fillmore College. I told him I still felt in crisis. I even blurted out the event of my brother's death and my inability to fill that void.

He paused after I finished as though he was laying a framework for a response. Harold spoke as though he were giving a lecture. He said that the existentialist and scientific rationalists had skewed the picture for students.

He wagged his finger at me. "There is no reason to suffer with all that we know." He sat back in his chair, both arms stretched out to his sides, looking like an old testament prophet. "You're in the right place this afternoon." He rose from his chair. "Those peanut-brained scientific rationalists--what narcissistic idiots! They don't know how strong our case is!"

"Which is what?" I asked, not certain how hard I could push.

"There are two arguments that squish those Lilliputian minds." Harold pursed his lips. "First, the mystical experience is incontrovertible. Five thousand years of history from Christianity, Judaism, Hinduism, Buddhism and Islam--all validate the reality."

The second argument, he said, was that the scientific mode of thinking was flawed. "The empirical method limits itself," he said, "only to what can be observed and measured. There is more to reality than the five senses."

He waved both hands, brandishing his pipe like a small sword. "Transcendence," he said, "incorporates all ways of knowing: rationality, intuition, the senses, feelings and thinking. By comparison rationalism is, at best, a brass quartet. Transcendence is the whole orchestra."

I sat back, relaxed and smiling. Here was Dr. Harold Menninger, in his book-filled library, advocating with equal doses of passion and reason, a view that for me was life-affirming. I loved his certainty and could feel a door open.

"Camus and Sartre," he almost spat the names, "are such midgets. They locked themselves in the bathroom of a great mansion. They stayed there so long they were reduced to playing in their own excrement." He stomped his foot as though he had just shaken the mansion free of feces, and Thelma and I applauded.

Now I could see where some of Thelma's emotion originated. The Menninger genes were wired for high voltage in both thought and feeling. Harold smiled and grabbed Marion's hand.

Thelma spoke up. “Uncle Harold, you’re getting too serious. Allen frets about his meaning all the time. He needs to have more fun.” Thelma grabbed my arm as if to ward off any remaining existential virus.

Harold laughed. “Yes, I’ve been terminally serious for a long time, too, but I think Allen--with your help, will find the balance.”

During the next few days I felt the imprint of Harold’s message. Mysticism might be the path that would thread things together. Professor Niels had never shared these ideas. Uncle Harold had presented me with a precious jewel.

CHAPTER 10

I spent the rest of July and early August working on the make-up papers I was assigned to write. This was part of the arrangement my parents had negotiated with the college in order for me to be readmitted. In late August, I got a terse letter from President Tyler saying I'd fulfilled my agreement. Mom and Dad were relieved. Dad wrote a letter to Tyler thanking him.

I didn't sleep well the week before my return. I worried that the students and faculty would view my takeover of Townsend Tower as bizarre. I also sweated over whether the basketball team would seek revenge. Thelma and I drove back together. I was surprised when I walked into the student union with Thelma and found every third or fourth student nodding, smiling, or greeting me by name.

Chad Stevens, the editor of the newspaper, sat at our table and bought us Cokes. He said I should run for one of the open student council seats. "You'd win hands down--a lot of students have identified with you."

On our way out, Dr. Johnson, a history professor shook my hand. "I loved what you did last May. You shook things up--that's healthy."

Thelma and I left and walked towards the library. Everywhere we went people were saying hello to us. Thelma locked her hand tighter in my own. "It's like we're the first couple of M.F.C.: face it, we are a good looking couple." We continued walking in ascending rhapsody toward the library but our reverie shattered as we entered the quadrangle and saw President Tyler heading straight towards us, head bent, munching one of his purple popsicles. Thelma whispered, "God, he looks just like Nixon." He spotted us, dropped his popsicle, and muttered under his breath as we passed.

René, Ivan and I went out for pizza and beer. René announced he had fallen in love with an Argentinian foreign exchange student. Ivan told us he was considering changing his major to art and was busy painting a full length-abstract-portrait of himself. He suggested, half jokingly, that we paint Mandarin Chinese graffiti on President Tyler's house as our final political act. I reminded him that he was the only student on campus who knew the language.

The three of us agreed to disband the Philosophers' Club. Ivan said all organizations follow a life cycle and our work was done. I watched Ivan gobble down the last slice of pizza. I looked at my compatriots of the last two years and remembered how they faded away the day I seized the tower.

At nine in the morning my dorm room door swung open. Larry Erskine stomped in followed by Ty-Ty. Behind them, in single file, entered all the members of the basketball team. They were all wearing chinos and white tee shirts.

I counted sixteen of my wished-for Galapagos exiles in my room. Some were sitting down on the beds and some leaned against the wall. Overall they had formed a semi-circle around me. I was a cornered prey.

Larry Erskine put his hands on his hips. "At dinner yesterday I overheard your little faggot buddy Pritchard bragging about how you guys wrote the underground newspaper. Between that and your speech last year, we got a score to settle."

My mouth felt full of cotton balls, as Ty-Ty stuck his face in mine, his breath evoking images of soldiers hit by mustard gas. "Fucking faggot--you humiliated us with that newspaper."

Larry pulled Ty away from me. "So, Ford, does the pen feel mightier than the sword today?"

"No," I said and I scanned the room. Everyone was bigger than me. My one hundred and forty pound, five nine frame, felt fragile.

Bob Hanscomb pulled out some of my clothes from my closet. He held up a Harris tweed sports jacket to show the group. "Not bad for a poor minister's son."

Ty-Ty grabbed my picture of Thelma. "Hey, we hear you're getting a lot of action from your babe." He put the picture close near his pelvis and gyrated his hips. "Ooh, Thelma, you're so hot..."

Something bolted out of me--it felt like a piece of Martin. I stood up and stepped towards Ty-Ty. "Look, you or anyone else can beat the shit out of me." My voice broke.

Several team members laughed, but the connection inside me snapped back.

"I don't even know how to fight. I do know I have rights and you guys abused them with the shit you pulled in this dorm." I cleared my throat. "Okay, I'm scared--but you must be more scared--there are sixteen of you and one of me." I looked at Ty-Ty. I wanted to taunt him. "Go ahead, beat the crap out of me--but it'll backfire--big time."

Ty-Ty moved towards me, fists raised. The door opened and Mrs. Herlihy, our portly dorm mother, waddled into the room. "Shame on you, Ty-Ty and Larry. Why does the whole team have to gang up on Allen? Everyone go back to your rooms."

The team filed out with Bob Hanscomb saying, "You're an asshole radical who embarrassed the whole college. No one will vote for you." He slammed the door as he left.

Shaun McAdams entered a few moments later, glowing like a leprechaun that had found two pots of gold. He'd seen the team enter our room and he'd raced to get Mom Herlihy.

I won a student council seat by a comfortable margin. On the morning following the election, Bill Hart, the current Student Council president, sat down at my table during breakfast. He said he could secure the necessary votes so I would be the next president.

"Ford, people are still talking about what you did. Your stunt was unique--you have a following. You can use that to push through progressive goals." He added that the other candidate was Bob Hanscomb, whom he felt was a lightweight. However, he cautioned me that Hanscomb was popular with some of the members and the election could be close. One week later, I had my first council meeting.

By an eleven to nine vote, I defeated Hanscomb. Thelma was thrilled. "Now I really do feel like the First Lady of Millard Fillmore College." I called Mom and Dad but both of their responses were tepid. Dad was worried I'd become embroiled in controversy again.

I returned to my room that night and held up the picture of Martin under the light. I was now six years older than my brother was in his sophomore year photo. His grin told me, once more, that anything was possible.

One of the strangest things that happened to me in my new leadership role was that I befriended President Tyler, whom I heard was furious about my election. For our first meeting, I felt inspired and brought him a box of one dozen purple, Hood popsicles. We talked that afternoon for two hours and he told me about the meddling of the Board of Trustees, and the fifty-year-old heating plant and how there was no money for the half-million dollars of urgent repairs. He also shared that we were losing good professors to higher paying colleges. Near the end of our meeting, in a quiet voice, he said that he hated the college's name too. "Let's face it," he said, "Millard Fillmore was a loser."

Just before I left he retrieved one of the popsicles from his office refrigerator and handed me half of it. We ended the meeting slurping and smiling at each other.

Overall, my senior year at M.F.C. was excellent. In my role of Student Council President, I pushed through several reforms in student government. First, we got regular faculty evaluations. Next, we got an exam week. And we got Buzz Frick to retire early. I even went to his retirement dinner. I made the Dean's List both semesters; I was feeling purpose.

My only discomfort was coming from Thelma. Throughout our senior year she kept ratcheting up the idea of marriage and whenever she did I'd notice a quivery feeling in my stomach. I'd put Thelma off by telling her we needed to graduate first, but as spring came I started to resist less.

CHAPTER 11

One month after graduation, Thelma and I married. The wedding was minimalist with only a Justice of the Peace and Harold and Marion present. Both sets of parents were not invited because they had expressed serious doubts about our betrothal. I had invited both René and Ivan, who lived in New Jersey, but they said they had conflicts.

Ollie hesitated but agreed to be my best man, stuttering before he said yes. However, two nights before the wedding, his mother called saying he had come down with the flu.

On the night before, I awoke at three in the morning with an upset stomach. I spent an hour pacing. I'd run out of reasons to put Thelma's request off and I kept recalling what Harold had said to me that morning privately--in his library.

"I've never seen Thelma so happy. All her other relationships never lasted more than three months. Please promise me you will go the distance with her." He added that he knew her mood swings were difficult but felt we had a chance to succeed.

Thelma and I went to Bermuda on a week long honeymoon. We'd pooled our savings of eleven hundred dollars and stayed at the premier hotel, the Hamilton House. Around two in the morning, I heard Thelma crying.

"What's wrong babe?" I asked.

"I don't believe I did this."

"What?"

"I never should've married you...I made a terrible mistake! I want it annulled in the morning." The crying and lamentation went on for another half an hour.

Body-slammed by her words, I went out on the balcony to get air. An hour later I returned to the room. I got into bed beside her, but lay with my back against hers. My sleep was fitful and ragged as I recycled Thelma's words in a series of jagged dream fragments.

I awoke when the morning sun poured into the room. I turned over and nudged Thelma awake. My voice quivered as I asked her what she wanted.

"Oh no! I could never leave you! It was the champagne... and I was tired." She kissed and hugged me a dozen times. We made love that day three times.

The rest of the honeymoon was a bliss ride. We rented motorbikes and explored the island's many small beaches and coves. Thelma was delighted with the pink sand, the swimming, and the snorkeling. During the last three days, we spent hours flying kites together on an isolated bluff.

At times I ran out of energy, but Thelma insisted on staying up till midnight. In bed on our last night, she rested her head on my chest. "Let's stay here forever." She cried hard as I held her until sleep closed her eyes.

We returned to our apartment in New York City riding on our honeymoon wave. We both felt the upgraded status of our new commitment. Still, I wasn't relaxed; part of me was edgy wondering what would come next from Thelma. Our relationship mimicked a roller coaster ride. There were steady accelerations, with great views from the high points, followed by sudden descents and hairpin turns. And there were moments when the train jumped off the tracks.

My time was soon taken up with my doctoral program at the New School for Social Sciences in New York City. The program was interdisciplinary and combined psychology and religion. At last I'd clarity about my vocation: I'd be a college teacher, one who gave hope and purpose to his students. Somehow, from this, Martin's dream would evolve.

Thelma coasted on our honeymoon high during our first month back. Her first project involved decorating our third floor in-law apartment which Harold and Marion had given us--rent free.

Besides the living room, bedroom, and kitchenette, there was a tiny room that would be my study. Thelma and I painted the apartment in a week. Bright yellows, blues and greens, and plants transformed the space and reflected Thelma's knack for colors. We found a brass bed and bureau in a second hand store, and Harold and Marion gave us a white wicker sofa and chair from their cellar. We were proud of our Lilliputian but elegant apartment.

New York City in the summer of 1972 was like a bubbling stew. There were Trotskyites, transvestites and transcendental meditators. Hippies were everywhere with long hair, love beads, and raucous life energy. I even watched my first gay pride march. Every Friday night, Thelma and I would sit by the Washington Square Monument in Greenwich Village and watch the whole city snake dance by us.

We got involved in the McGovern for President campaign, registering new voters and working the phone bank at headquarters. On election day in November, we stood in the rain all day outside the local voting site with our McGovern signs. There was an energy charge that was reconnecting me to Martin's dream. Someday, I repeated to myself, there would be another serious campaign.

Despite the fact McGovern lost, life was getting better. My doctoral dissertation topic on peak experiences and mysticism was approved by my committee. My rational and intuitive sides were connecting as I did my readings and research. My life plan was positioned in a target scope, and I was moving towards it at a steady clip.

Our first visit as a married couple to my parents' house was brief. First, Thelma confronted my father about his support for Nixon. At dinner, she complained that my parents used iceberg lettuce instead of romaine. And twice she pulled me into the pantry to complain about my mother's coldness. My father's last comment to me in his study was, "You blew it by not going into the ministry. Now you're in a flaky doctoral program in an overcrowded field." We cut the three day visit short and left the next morning.

I threw myself into my graduate studies. My favorite professor was William Starbird, a man in his late forties who had been a veteran, businessman and Trappist Monk. He had left the order evolving his own blend of pantheism and paganism, which he called pagtheism. We were all invited to parties at his house where we drank, danced, smoked pot--and debated. I respected Starbird until Thelma told me he groped her in the kitchen while I was in the living room arguing against Pascal's Wager. I withdrew from his classes.

Thelma got a full-time job teaching art at a private school and became the major breadwinner. However, complaints came fast from my teacher-wife about her students' behavior. Her contract wasn't renewed at the end of the year. Thelma was surprised--I wasn't. Fortunately, she found another art teacher position through a contact from Uncle Harold.

After one year of marriage, it was clear I'd married three women. The first I named Doris Day. The one I fell in love with, she was beautiful, sexy, talented and upbeat. She could paint a picture in an afternoon, create a gourmet meal in the evening, and party to midnight. The clue to Doris was the color of her clothing. She wore shades of teal, blue and burgundy. Doris, the All-American Girl, lived with us four or five days a week and was always riding on a whirlwind of energy.

One day each week, I would run into Attila--usually on Sundays. The key to identifying the warrior-princess was her clenched mouth, wrinkled forehead, and piercing stares. Attila would strike hard and fast--then disappear.

One January night in bed, I felt a sharp elbow jab in my ribs and heard a battlefield shout. "You fucking bastard, you've got all the covers!"

Dazed, I threw all the bedding in her direction. I stumbled into the living room, grabbed a blanket, and wrapped myself in it. I felt like one of those wretched Indians you see outside the saloon. The next morning I confronted Doris who was in the kitchen.

"Oh, I'd never do anything like that honey; you must've been dreaming." She laughed and smiled, and said, "What do you want for breakfast?"

Norma was the third. She gave herself away by her drab browns and the fact that she slept late. She behaved like an indentured servant trapped in a long-term contract. I usually encountered her on weekends. It would take her hours to do simple tasks; and sometimes she would spend the whole afternoon staring out the window or taking naps.

In my second year of the doctoral program, I became a teaching assistant and taught my first psychology class. I encouraged my students to express their feelings in weekly reaction papers and to do autobiographies as their major paper. The evaluations at the end of the class were laudatory. My career choice was solid.

I joined a weekly encounter group at the graduate school led by Dr. Tim Babbitt. There were ten of us in the group and we met once a week for the school year. Babbitt, in his late thirties, was articulate and confrontive.

"Ford, you don't feel--you intellectualize everything." Members of the group agreed, and one by one, gave me examples where I'd talked about feelings, but didn't show them. I broke down and cried, talking about Martin, my search and my inability to find a new brother. It was the first time I'd cried since my mother announced her atheism, five years earlier.

"You've got some real work to do," Babbitt told me, and he shook his head. I heard him but I didn't hear him. I got home at ten that night, went to my study, and put Martin's picture in my bottom bureau drawer. I also took the book on Rasputin off my shelf and stuffed it in the same drawer.

Thelma's second year as an art teacher was stormy. She complained about either the administration, the immature students, or interfering parents. One day in February, I came home at eleven in the morning and found her lying on the sofa, bawling.

"What's wrong, babe?" I asked.

"It's terrible! It's terrible!"

"What?

"I've been suspended!"

"What for?"

"I yelled at Tommy Becker and they sent me home. Imagine that!"

The full story came out later. Tommy had dipped a paper airplane into some red paint and thrown it at a female student, smearing her new, white, silk blouse. The girl yelled and knocked over her art easel, which, in turn, sprayed paint on a dozen of her classmates.

Attila had then commanded the boy: "You fucking little bastard--you're banished from this class!" Thelma was fired two days later.

She took a month off and then took a job as a waitress at Gus and Bill's deli. She lasted the whole year without a problem except for one water pitcher spill, which she insisted was an accident.

Despite the hassles of my marriage to Thelma, I was continually gifted by Harold's wisdom and generosity. He took no rent and was always inviting us for meals. My favorite ritual was Sunday night when, after dinner, he and I would retreat to his paneled library, where we would smoke cigars and sip brandy. Usually, there would be a crackling fire behind us.

"Now, about your studies this week." Harold would intersperse his question with a flawless smoke ring. "We need the symbol of infinity to bless our discussions."

Everything was open for discussion. We talked about philosophy, politics, theology, and history. Frequently, I'd ask him to repeat the story of his visit to the legendary Jewish fortress of Masada in Israel. He'd been twenty-four at the time and had left his tour group. He loved to tell the details of his awakening from "secular slumber," as he put it.

"It was dusk," he said. "I was standing near the East Side wall, *Bam!* It hit me. Right out of nowhere. I was catapulted out of my normal reality. Unbelievable!" Harold said he could see, hear, taste, and feel--in a new way. He compared it to a peek through a cosmic keyhole. *"I saw everything for the first time."*

Harold pounded the arm of his chair, his expression joyful. "There is this overwhelming experience of love at the core of everything." This was followed by another pound on the chair arm like an old testament prophet proclaiming the final revelation.

Noticing my grimace Harold said, "Allen, you need to be patient, the experience will come to you. Patience."

I nodded and smiled. Inside though, I could feel the hungry, snarling animal that was craving the sacred soul meal. And I could hear the doubts of the skeptic. Nothing that good could be true.

One Sunday I blurted out my worst fear: "What if the universe is a random event...a joke? The idea scares the hell out of me."

Harold puffed on his cigar several times. "Sometimes I wonder if your search is more emotional than intellectual. I sense this anguished part of you unable to trust life." He blew another smoke ring, then sipped his brandy. He studied my eyes.

I went silent. My throat tightened and I fought the impulse to cry. "You're touching something." I squirmed in my chair.

He puffed again. "I sense that stuck part wants a high degree of certainty?"

I laughed. "Yes, the expectations are high." Then I told Harold I was afraid to count on any certainty. Worse, there was the fear that if I chose a set of beliefs it could be the wrong set. "I'm scared of rolling my dice--my one chance--and screwing up big time."

"You're afraid you might be the first one in history to make that mistake. My, you're important."

I swallowed. I felt foolish and fragile.

Harold smiled again sensing that my armor was dissolving. "I wish you could find that extra certainty. But I'm afraid it's not there. Your father is right about one thing."

"What?"

"At some point the rational arguments falter and there has to be a leap of faith--Kierkegard was right."

Harold winked at me. "If you train properly you could achieve the goal. It isn't a chasm." He laughed.

Despite our growing closeness the skeptic in me would still surface and badger Harold. "Define the nature of God." Harold gave me an extended description mentioning sunsets, Mozart, and making love. I told him that his arguments were all emotional ones.

Harold scowled. "Your labeling of my examples as emotional arguments is a linguistic trap. I could fill the room--twice--with books documenting my case but you'd still want more. Your need for certainty implodes upon itself."

Bile rose in my mouth. "Explain how a just God allowed those dogs to kill my brother." I had both shouted the question and pounded the chair arm and I was trembling.

Harold leaned back in his chair, put his cigar down, clasped his hands and closed his eyes. He went silent. A minute went by. I stood up to leave the room. "Sit down!" he shouted. He stood. His body seemed compressed and tight, his eyes glistening. He took out his handkerchief and blew his nose.

"You ask the most wrenching of questions: Why does suffering happen? We Jews have conducted an ongoing seminar on the subject for four thousand years." He sighed, and relit his cigar, using it to underscore the importance of his remarks: "I think I have an answer--granted, a crude one." He cleared his throat. "Tragedies like your brother's represent the ultimate paradox. In this reality, what happened was abominable...beyond words. Yet, there is another reality that envelops this one in which there is quite another meaning. I feel this more than I can explain it."

"I resist paradox," I said.

"Yes," he said. "I see that well."

We finished our cigars in a long silence.

By doing additional course work all three summers, I was able to finish my doctoral program in three years. Harold's support and my focus on transcendence and peak experience left me in a state of convergence and unity.

During my doctoral studies, I'd stayed in touch with my friends by reading the *Millard Fillmore Alumni Magazine.* René Prichard had moved to Argentina, married his girlfriend, and gone into banking. Ivan was in a doctoral program in Linguistics at Princeton and still working on his autobiography. And Shaun McAdams, who had married his hometown sweetheart, was teaching biology at his former high school.

I was in frequent communication with Ollie, who was finishing a doctoral program in American History. He was still complaining about either his height, his stuttering or his lack of a girlfriend. Strangely, he'd decided to do his doctoral dissertation on Millard Fillmore's Presidency.

During this time, I was having a recurring dream about Rasputin. This time I was back in the parsonage at Greenfield, in my old bedroom. I could hear someone in Martin's room. I would look through the keyhole of the locked door, and I could see Rasputin sitting at Martin's desk. He ignored my pleas and knocking, and kept his back to me.

CHAPTER 12

Once I had my doctorate my game plan was to use the influence of a family friend to open the door to college teaching. Winston Northrup was Academic Vice President of Chesterton University, and he'd hinted that he could get me on the short list for faculty openings. I wanted to be near home, yet have space from my parents.

Chesterton University was located in Westbridge, Connecticut, a city of forty thousand. The community was prosperous and had a distinguished history. There was both a naval base and a variety of industries.

I applied for a position as an assistant professor. My grades were good and my recommendations solid. I was relaxed and confident during the interview with the five member selection committee.

Three weeks later, I was offered the position. However, there was some opposition from the Dean of the Liberal Arts Department, Sydney Hammond III. I learned, through the grapevine, that the Dean had derided my dissertation topic of peak experiences, as well as the nature of my interdisciplinary program. I was startled because this was the same Sydney Hammond that wrote about Rasputin in his now renown book.

Thelma decided to capitalize on our move by making a career change. She wanted to sell real estate, believing that the combination of her art background and outgoing personality, would be an asset. She also began studies with a local astrologer by the name of Quintin Barrows. Before long she filled the den up with charts, books and pamphlets. I made cracks about astrology, which led to several fiery arguments. In response Thelma moved all her astrology materials from our den into an attic room and informed me my presence was forbidden there.

We'd bought an old victorian on the south side of Westbridge. The two of us had a good time that summer choosing paint colors for the outside and lining up contractors for the interior projects. Then Thelma began to push for a baby--and I resisted. "We need time," I said. "Both of us starting new jobs and we've got the house to finish and student debts to pay off."

She crossed her arms and tapped her foot. "Okay. You get one more year." The fact that her astrologer said August would be an ideal time to get pregnant since the asteroid Chiron was entering her twelfth house, contributed to the problem.

Despite astrology, our first year in Westbridge was productive. I was only six years older than many of my students and felt an easy rapport with them. Thelma got her real estate license and sold three houses before she blew up at one of her customers for backing out of a sale.

My one problem at work continued to be Dean Hammond. At the first college cocktail party, I made the mistake of asking him about Rasputin. He dismissed my inquiry by saying that too much attention had been focused on the gang leader. I disagreed and got into an argument.

Winston shook his head when he heard of my encounter. "Not a good move for someone who needs tenure."

Overall, I was offended by Sydney's views. He was a determinist. His world view saw humanity controlled by a combination of unconscious forces and environmental factors. At thirty-eight he was frank that he intended to be either a college president or run for an important political office before he was forty-five.

My problems with Hammond escalated after I attended Winston Northrup's sixtieth party. As we entered Winston's foyer I was surprised to find Sydney Hammond standing there.

"Here he comes...the resident humanist who believes in innate goodness and mystical states."

I locked eyes with Sydney. Thelma squeezed my hand and pulled me into the solarium; I got a rum and coke and downed it in one extended gulp. Thelma fell into one of her Doris moods, chatting with everyone and asking people about their birth signs. Throughout the evening, I kept going out of my way to avoid Sydney. As soon as he entered a room, I would move into another. However, after three drinks part of me wanted a showdown, and I wandered back into the library.

A discussion was going on about Vietnam. I launched in with my opinion, unaware that Sydney had entered the room behind me. "Vietnam was a tragic mistake," I said. "There are other viable alternatives to war."

"Well, the idealist is at it again. Why can't you do-gooders see the big picture?" Hammond went on to say that war was inherent in the human condition and had beneficial effects. "Most of the people drafted were from the lower socio-economic level...so the gene pool gets flushed out--big deal."

The group there smiled nervously at Hammond. All were connected, in some way, with the university and knew his reputation. "After all," he said, "this is a random universe. Why are we all so serious?"

"I disagree," I said. "The universe has purpose. Human nature is positive. There are societies that exist without warfare."

"There you go again, touting piddily exceptions," said Sydney.

I countered by citing Maslow and Rogers. "And they believe we have free choice and that we are driven by needs for belonging and actualization."

"Here we go, more feel-good hype from the touchie-feelie crowd whose beliefs are backed by few hard studies."

I rebutted the argument stating that the United States was founded by immigrants, paupers and jailbirds. "By the way, Sydney, some of these people were probably your ancestors."

"Thank you, you've just given me my best argument. Let's look at American society--now." Sydney countered with extended analysis of how all our current social indicators had worsened.

"You're exaggerating those trends to fit your book's thesis."

"All my statements are verifiable--are yours?"

"Maslow's studies on self-actualizing people are valid in my opinion." My stomach was churning but I kept my exterior controlled.

"Anecdotal reports and subjective experiences are not verifiable science. The hard proof is not there."

"I suppose your book about ten street gang leaders was an example of large representative sampling. And, c'mon, Sydney--why couldn't you track down Rasputin? Where is he? He could be alive somewhere doing good things and that would contradict your book's thesis."

"Bullshit!" Sydney shouted. "Rasputin is dead or in prison. Not one gang leader I studied broke out."

"Prove it Sydney! Where is he?"

Sydney became quiet, his eyes fixed on mine. I could tell I'd drawn blood.

"Rasputin wasn't that important in the scheme of things," he said.

"Some of your critics disagreed. If Rasputin is alive, that could shoot a gaping hole in your determinism. And it would also make a case for free will."

"Ah, the minister's son and his notions of Christian free-will. Now there's a popular superstition."

"I believe it's real." I felt my throat tighten.

"So was it free will that guided you when you watched those dogs kill your brother?"

I could feel my lip trembling and my legs shaking but I couldn't move. Sydney and I were in the center of the circle. I felt like a deaf mute and ached for Martin to be at my side--he'd say the perfect thing.

Then Thelma broke through the circle, grabbed my arm and pulled me towards the door.

Sydney made one final comment as I left. "Well, once more, young Lochinvar has broken his lance--again--on the parapets of rational science. Perhaps we should consider transferring him to the English department. He could teach the Romantic Poets there." I heard a number of people laugh.

Thelma squeezed my upper arm as she walked me out the doors. "I hate that pompous bastard! I almost threw my drink on him. He was deliberately humiliating you in front of your peers."

"Allen! There you are." Winston Northrop was walking toward us sounding out of breath. "I caught the tail end of your debate...it was quite a mutual thrashing."

"I feel like I've soured your party--I'm sorry."

"I must be frank. The two of you have this way of igniting one another. It's not good for the institution."

I frowned and Winston turned his attention to his flowers. "Now look at these roses. I have been nurturing these miniatures for over fifteen years. Smell them." He took a long, peaceful inhale. "Ah...yes, if we could get the people of the world to plant, nurture, and smell roses, we might advance the human condition. I think both you and Sydney should take up the practice."

"Somehow," I said, "I believe Sydney's roses would have more thorns."

Winston shook his head and walked back towards the house.

I awoke at three in the morning and shuffled into the den, where I sat in my brown leather chair. How had Hammond found out? The tumblers in my head were now lining up: Thelma had been the source for Hammond's knowledge, somehow.

The next morning, while walking on the beach, I confronted Thelma. She cried and apologized a dozen times. She had revealed the information to Andrea, wife of Sydney Hammond, at a previous faculty party. I said nothing as we drove home.

I slept in the guest room that night.

CHAPTER 13

Later that summer, when Thelma and I were painting the outside of our home, we realized our ladder was too short for the higher places. I remembered that family friends had relocated from Greenfield to a street four blocks away. Ralph and Betty Hughes were retired but I had seen Ralph painting their house several months earlier, so I knocked on their door and Betty greeted me. She said I could borrow the ladder which was in the backyard.

"Zlavik, my son-in-law, is out there target practicing with his bow. Ask him to help you."

I entered the backyard and saw a tall, well-built man, my age, dressed in khakis and a green polo shirt, leaning over a stuffed archery target studying the configuration of arrows.

He turned around quickly when he heard my hello. His face looked grey and tense but shifted into a smile upon sighting me.

"You're not a Jehovah's Witness, are you?"

"No, but I did sell encyclopedias once--I lasted a week."

Zlavik laughed. "Then we have something in common. But I lasted longer." His whole demeanor had changed during our short exchange. His color was better, and his whole body had loosened up.

I had a strange feeling, a sense that I knew him, but dismissed it.

"Your mother-in-law sent me out here. I want to borrow their ladder."

"Sure. How can I help?"

"I live about four blocks away. Are you up for a short walk?"

"Hey, I'm getting bored playing Robin Hood, let's do it," he said, and we trudged the distance back to my house. Conversation flowed as we joked about being mistaken for either firemen or house painters.

I invited Zlavik and his wife Barbara to our home that following Saturday for a cookout. We were all in our middle twenties and liked The Grateful Dead, Simon and Garfunkel and wished we'd gone to Woodstock. Barbara and I reminisced about when she and her parents had lived in Greenfield and went to my father's church. After a month the four of us were seeing each other socially at least once a week.

I discovered that Thelma was impressed with Zlavik when I overheard a conversation with her sister, Anna. "This new friend of ours should be in the movies with his looks. He's six two, with black hair, and he has these beautiful, cobalt blue eyes. Plus he pulls you in with this incredible smile."

Barbara and Zlavik were an odd match. Barbara was attractive but an introvert and content to remain a legal secretary even though she might have been a lawyer. Zlavik in contrast, spoke as if there were no ceiling on what he could do.

During one visit, Zlavik noticed my distress from a sore throat. "May I try something?" he asked. His voice was soft but confident.

I stiffened in my seat. "I don't believe in folk remedies." "Allen," Barbara said, "Zlavik has a gift with his hands--let him try."

"Okay," I said, though I was skeptical.

"Sit down on that chair I'll stand behind you and place my hand on your throat--just stay relaxed."

I complied. Zlavik's large left hand wrapped gently around one side of my throat, while his other hand encircled the other side. He kept his hands in position for several minutes and I felt heat coming from both his palms. Next, I experienced a popping sensation in my throat--and the tightness was gone.

"Where did you learn that?" I asked.

"Just picked it up--no big deal."

It was the same evening Thelma asked Zlavik the origin of his name. He grinned and told us about his Uncle David Kettner, who he had lived with every summer, from age thirteen through seventeen. David used the summers to tutor Zlavik in a variety of spiritual disciplines including archery, yoga, and meditation. Zlavik said the name came from an obscure, tenth century Hungarian King and hero, by the name of "Zlavik the Great." The king had freed his country in a war where the opposing armies far outnumbered his own. Shortly afterward the king disappeared, baffling his subjects and future historians.

David dreamed that his sister's first born should be named after the hero because he, too, would do important things for his country. Zlavik added the fact that his uncle was an eccentric alcoholic. "Despite those things, he was both a father figure and an incredible teacher."

A few months into our friendship, Zlavik divulged that he had a disorder similar to epilepsy. He took medication, but the condition was unpredictable at times, manifesting in seizures and blackouts. I noticed Zlavik drumming his fingers as he talked about the problem. He said he didn't want us startled if he had an episode.

One month later, during one of our get-togethers, Zlavik complained that he was feeling faint. Barbara took him to our bedroom to lay down. She returned in minutes and said he'd blacked out. "He should rest for about half an hour." Barbara was calm, but Thelma looked as tense as I felt.

Barbara sighed. "They really don't know what the condition is." She said that one doctor believed it was a rare allergy, and another said it was caused by brain damage at birth. Zlavik got furious at one doctor who suggested it might be psychosomatic. She told us that they had consulted a variety of experts, but no one was certain. Zlavik believed it had been caused by a fall from a motorcycle while he'd been in the army.

After twenty minutes, all three of us went to check on Zlavik. Barbara walked in first, but backed out--fast. "I need your help. Sometimes he comes out of the blackouts disoriented and fearful. Stay in the background...I need to reassure him."

She re-entered the room, moving slowly. Zlavik was on the middle of the bed, on all fours making a low, growling noise.

"It's okay...it's me," Barbara said. "It's okay, honey. You'll be okay." She placed a hand on his shoulder.

A shudder ran through Zlavik's body. Barbara began rubbing his back in a clockwise circle pattern, gently increasing the radius.

"You're safe here, no one will hurt you...we'll get you home soon. You'll be okay." She continued rubbing Zlavik's back.

Thelma and I backed up against the doorway. Zlavik's face began to soften.

"Zlavik," Barbara said, "can you try standing up? Here, use the wall to steady yourself."

Zlavik tried to steady himself against the wall. Barbara took his right arm and slung it over her shoulder and the two of them walked out of the bedroom and towards the back door, Zlavik's expression was blank. There was no awareness of where or who he was.

As soon as the door closed Thelma said, “My God! He was like a zombie!” She stood with her arms folded, her back pressed against the kitchen counter. “The thing was so bizarre. And that growling noise, my God.” She shot me a look. “Don’t you dare compare my mood shifts to Zlavik’s--it’s not the same.”

CHAPTER 14

A smiling Zlavik sauntered into Jackson's Restaurant precisely at two o'clock. He briefly flirted with the cashier and waved to a few people before he moved toward me. As he dropped into the booth, he apologized briefly for the blackout, then said "Hey, I want to tell you about a new cost-saving plan I'm proposing at work."

Zlavik had gotten a job at our city's largest employer, the Cabot Insurance Company. He opened a napkin and began to fill it with facts, figures and cost projections that would save the company several million by switching to an in-house healthcare system.

I watched like someone with a split-screen television. On one screen was the growling feral creature that had taken over my bedroom; on the other, was the "All American boy." By the time Zlavik had finished his blueberry pie and coffee, he'd covered three more napkins with charts and figures.

"Watch them eat up this proposal...there'll be a promotion in it for me." He leaned back in the booth, arms stretched across the top of the bench.

I nodded. "Sounds good." I remembered that Martin and I had once sat in the same booth.

During the next six months, I managed to piece together the full story of Zlavik's seizure disorder. Barbara shared some information, but Zlavik was surprisingly candid in our conversations. He said he fell off a motorcycle in Japan, while in the army. After a short treatment period, the Army discharged him. Zlavik stayed with his mother in Seattle as the seizures worsened, and he was hospitalized for a month.

"I could feel the different medications interacting and they spun me into a depression. I was asleep in the hospital bed when these two gorillas marched in and flashed a piece of paper. 'It's a court order,' they said. 'We've come to take you to the state hospital.' No pun intended, I just went nuts."

Zlavik said the two weeks in the hospital were awful, saying the place was from *One Flew Over the Cuckoo's Nest.* His Uncle David managed to get him out.

I nodded. "I got sent to a psychiatric hospital when I was in college." I laughed. Zlavik's eyebrows raised. "I was also sent away because of a seizure disorder." I related the story of the Townsend Tower takeover. I also shared the confusion and pain of my search.

"Man, you've been hustling for your truth."

"Thanks."

I leaned forward in the booth and told Zlavik about Martin's death. I surprised myself and confessed my inability to move and use the Bowie knife.

Zlavik's eyes widened as I finished the tale. He shook his head and sighed. "I'm so sorry."

I nodded.

"We've both been through a lot...we have things in common...."

"Yeah." I leaned back in the booth.

Zlavik paused. "Where are you today?"

I explained how Uncle Harold and my doctoral studies had given me a home port. "Some things are still missing--I can't quite put my finger on it."

"Do you miss your brother?"

"Everyday."

"I never had a brother--it must have been great." He looked at me for a long time. I looked away.

Two months later during one of our meetings at Jackson's, Zlavik drummed his fingers against the table. "You've never had one of those mystical experiences-–right?"

"Some little things," I said. "No breakouts."

"I don't want to give away the store, but I think I can be of help." He laughed. "Man, you wouldn't believe the places I've been." He added that he would share more with me at a later time.

My new friend was easy to talk with. He didn't judge, even when I hinted that I might have set up Martin. "You were twelve-–anyone could choke in that situation." During our conversations Zlavik gave me his total attention. He'd nod his head and his eyes would dart to the right and then back like he was recording the conversation. He never interrupted. By the end of our first year we had established a ritual of meeting every Saturday afternoon. In may ways it became the highlight of my week.

During one of our Saturday afternoon rituals I remembered Zlavik had lived in LA for a while, and I asked him if he'd heard of Rasputin--and he spilled coffee at the mention of Rasputin's name. "How do you know about him?"

I told him about Hammond's book and his emphasis on Rasputin. I even told him about wanting to meet him.

"He was a bad dude. You don't want to know him."

"What happened to him?"

"I heard he died of a drug overdose." Zlavik said he wanted to borrow the book from me. He ended our conversation that day earlier than usual.

One month later Zlavik and I were sitting at our booth in Jackson's. The conversation was in a lull, and Zlavik scanned the nearby booths. "I need to talk to you about something."

"What?" I said.

"This is difficult, but I, hear a voice." Zlavik again looked to see if anyone was sitting close by.

I studied Zlavik. He was making steady eye contact. I found myself both intrigued and repelled.

"What's it like?" I finally asked.

Zlavik rolled his eyes. "There's an overwhelming energy surge. For several seconds I feel like I'm being taken over by a presence. What stands out is the authority--it's striking."

I observed Zlavik's demeanor. He wasn't talking like a wild man, but like someone who might be drinking from a genuine sacred well.

"Are you testing me?" I asked.

"Yes," he smiled.

"So, do I pass muster?"

"As long as you don't get up and leave."

We both laughed.

"So, who's the voice?"

"It doesn't have a name." He grinned.

"I don't know what to say. How sure are you? Our minds are clever tricksters."

"The voltage is total--you just surrender." He leaned back. "I love how it feels. Every time it happens, I feel like I've gone home."

“Sounds like some kind of peak experience.”

He nodded, “Of course--there’s no other explanation.”

For the first time, I resented Zlavik. He seemed to have a spiritual connection that was both real and rare. I’d spent eight years knocking walls down for a touch of the sacred and Zlavik got his gift from a motorcycle fall. For a moment, I recalled the growling, feral creature on my bed but I pushed the image out.

“Tell me more,” I said.

“I access the voice by meditating but sometimes I hear the voice spontaneously. The voice spoke to me on my first date with Barbara. She went to the bathroom and the voice hit for about three seconds: ‘*Marry Barbara.*’ On the way home I told her we’d be getting married.” Barbara, he said, stammered, turned red, and almost wet her pants. “We’ve been married four years and things feel good.”

“What else has the voice said?”

He said the original message told him to meditate and evolve a fitness regime. Zlavik said the voice told him the practice would buttress him for his life’s mission.

“Did it tell you to come to the east coast?”

“Yes, I’m here on a quest of sorts.” He gave me a nervous smile.

“What was the last message?”

Zlavik’s face went grey. He drummed his fingers hard.

“The last message occurred the day before we first met.” He said he was agonizing over it when I first saw him in the backyard of his in-law’s house.

“What happened?”

“This is hard to talk about.” His eyes were moist, and he was rubbing the left side of his chest with his right hand.

“What is it?” I prodded.

“The message said I have eight years to complete three important tasks. The tasks are separate, but in some way interconnected. All three are to be accomplished in an outstanding way. If I don’t complete the tasks, my seizures will increase.”

“Any clues what the tasks are?”

“No. A year has gone by. I’ve asked for additional guidance, but I get nothing.”

“So the worst scenario is that you never complete the tasks and you have more seizures. Can you live with that?”

Zlavik began drumming with both hands. “There is one piece of information you don’t have.”

“What?” I held my breath.

Zlavik looked away, took a deep breath, and resumed eye contact. "I've recently seen the top neurologist in New Haven. The doctor said, at the rate the seizures are progressing, I'll be lucky to live past thirty-five. I'm twenty-eight now, and I'm not sure if I've even begun the tasks."

I shook my head and released my breath. "Whew."

"Oh, there is one other thing."

"What?"

"I got a clue in a meditation."

"Oh?"

"'*The healing is on the mountain of your knowing.*' Figure that one out."

I could feel myself backing into a corner of the booth. "Are you sure your psyche isn't setting you up? The message seems so extreme."

"I find a space in my meditations that tells me to let go...that I may be trying too hard. When I trust this, I sense there's a way out." He grinned, but it seemed forced.

I shook my head. "These three tasks sound like a spiritual 'Mission Impossible' to me."

"Barbara doesn't know what the neurologist said. I need your confidance on that. She worries enough."

I nodded.

"I'll help you anyway I can," I said. I was surprised at how the words had jumped out of me.

Zlavik smiled. "From the first day we met I knew that."

CHAPTER 15

Zlavik's unique outlet was archery, a skill Uncle David had taught him over their five summers. He enjoyed inviting people along and would wax eloquent about it's benefits. "I love it, the sport relaxes, renews me--it's a meditation."

During our second summer as friends, Zlavik insisted that I take up the sport. "Look, try it just once. If you don't like it, I won't pester you, but it's one of the great manly arts." I agreed to meet him at the Buckfield Archery Range one Sunday in June.

I decided to observe him before announcing my presence. Before each shot, Zlavik looked down at the ground and took several slow, deep breaths. He then placed the arrow in the bow, slowly leaned back and took another deep breath, seeming to merge his body with the bow and arrow.

"Whoosh." The arrow sailed into its target. I noticed all the previous arrows tightly clustered in the bullseye. Over and over, he repeated the process. Breathe, pause and release. All these elements came together in a seamless dance.

Zlavik sensed me. "Come on, it's your turn at bat."

I started to protest. "I feel like Friar Tuck competing against Robin Hood."

His voice and manner shifted. "Hey, this isn't about competition. Be a kid again--just play with the bow and arrows."

My first arrow missed by ten feet. I swore, then caught myself. I took several more breaths. The second arrow hit the outer edge.

"Good. You're loosening up. Let the shot come out of you--don't think about it." I practiced shooting for another half-hour. I could see myself improving. Zlavik kept nodding, smiling, and repeating, "You're getting there..."

I was pleased with the first lesson. The slow three breaths between each shot were the key. "Thanks for not teasing. I need to get my confidence up." Zlavik nodded. I remembered how Martin worked with me on my batting swing in the sixth grade. He'd used the same low voice tone.

On the way back to the parking lot, Zlavik was whistling and grinning. "Damn...Uncle David gave me one hell of an anchor with archery." He slapped me twice on the back before he got in his car.

Without thinking, I said, "Thanks, Bro." I blushed, catching what I'd said. Zlavik smiled and drove off.

One afternoon, at our corner booth at Jackson's Restaurant, Zlavik told me about his fitness regimen. He explained that, because of the seizure problem, he had to stay in top physical and mental condition. He said he got up early every morning, six days a week and meditated for forty-five minutes. "God," he said, "I get so high from it."

"How do you meditate?" I asked.

He said the first stage was focusing on the breath. He would repeat the number "one" each time he exhaled. The pattern was simple: in the nose, out the mouth, over and over again.

"The key is watching the breath. Hey, it's better than sex--how is that for an endorsement?"

"What happens next?"

"Great stuff." Zlavik said the next step was to switch from the breath to your thoughts. He said, one by one, you see your perceptions come and go. His Uncle David said monitoring your thoughts was like watching train boxcars--one right after another. "The trick was to switch from the boxcars to being an observer on the platform watching the cars."

"Anything else?"

"You start noticing that there are gaps between the boxcars...and you are able to go through them. Damn, it's an unbelievable space."

I leaned back. "That's a lot of work!"

"Oh there is one more thing," he added. "The final stage is you work at taking your moment to moment awareness into your everyday life. All day long, over and over again you bring that consciousness to your waking state. This, in turn, can lead to enlightenment."

Zlavik said his Uncle David believed this practice could transform the world. One by one people could wake up, and breath by breath we'd build a new world. He said the name of the practice was Vipassana meditation.

I smirked at Zlavik. "So are you enlightened?"

"No. But once in awhile I get my foot in the door. Meditation would be good for you," Zlavik said. "The practice will prepare you for those sacred places." He added that he had a crowded agenda over the next decade. "I hope I'm up for it."

I nodded, acknowledging his concern and registering the fact that he had emitted an extra long sigh.

"Allen, you might as well know my final secret. It might be a stretch for you, but try to stay open." Zlavik grimaced. "Okay--here goes." He said part of his predicament was that he was being stalked by a giant wolf. The creature appeared as a result of some esoteric practices he and his uncle had engaged in. "It could kill me if I'm not careful." He explained that only his Uncle David could help him, but no one knew where he went. "He disappeared after we had a bad argument."

"Jesus Christ! I don't know what to say." Zlavik's gaze remained calm as I pushed back against the wooden booth. I scanned his face, hoping that it was a joke, but he stared back. I drove home that afternoon trying to compute the element of the wolf. Zlavik, somehow, had manufactured his own boogeyman. A giant black wolf in the state of Connecticut was absurd.

Every year on Labor Day, Alice Forsyth, a colleague of mine in the Psychology Department, gave a party on the spacious lawn of her house, which fronted the Connecticut River. She usually invited sixty to eighty guests, children included.

She planned well. Her brother Mac would show up with a couple of his antique cars and give rides to the kids, and there were croquet sets, badminton, two canoes, and a row boat. The only downside was that Sidney Hammond usually attended.

I managed to get Zlavik invited to the event. He hit the jackpot with his introduction of an annual spitting contest for women.

At precisely three p.m., Alice rang a bell and asked everyone to form a circle. "The rumor you've been hearing is true. We're attempting to teach a special group of women the male art of spitting. Zlavik Johnson will be the coach."

Zlavik stepped into the center of the group. "Ladies and gentlemen, you're about to witness a historic event as we induct the first group of women into the secret school of manly spitting."

The crowd laughed and in response, six women rose to their feet and moved forward. There was Alice, Marion, Suzy Meyers, and three others whom I hadn't met. Zlavik began a short lecture, walking back and forth like a drill sergeant motivating a platoon for the front.

"Lesson number one is that there are three basic categories of spitting. First, was the common spit, which is usually projected onto sidewalks. The goal is to do it fast with a range of five to six feet and remember ladies, the common spit is done by puckering the mouth and simply blowing out a small amount of saliva. This is one way men mark their territory." He demonstrated category one, which elicited a groan from the audience.

"Next, we move up the ladder to a type of spitting known as 'the clam.'" He said the projectile must be at least twice the size of a common spit and should include some phlegm for texture and adhesion. "A little throat noise helps. The range is six to eight feet." He puckered up and spit. Another groan followed.

"Now, you're about to experience the crown jewel, the 'hawk.' This is twice the size of a 'clam' and the key, is to make a deep, long-lasting noise from the base of the throat, as you assemble a large glob." He executed a 'hawk' replete with extended guttural sounds.

Just then I noticed Thelma covering her mouth and running towards the house. I also noticed Sidney Hammond standing on the back porch with an intense look of scrutiny on his face. I walked off in another direction, to avoid him. Ollie was standing beside Hammond and he later said that Sidney had asked a lot of questions about Zlavik.

Zlavik remained undaunted. He lined up his volunteers. "Okay, this is not a charm school. Emily Post wouldn't approve. We're not spitting into a napkin here. The goal is to be crude and coarse."

The crowd laughed.

"Okay, ladies, we will wind up this event by doing a ten foot distance spit. No, Marion, you're dribbling. Start over Suzy, get back to the line."

After several tries, Alice and Suzy hit the ten-foot mark, and the crowd cheered.

Afterwards, Ollie pulled me aside. "Do you believe what that guy can do? He should have his own talk show. Hell, we could put him up against Johnny Carson." He laughed, shook his head, and went back to munching his hot dog. Ollie added that Sidney seemed agitated and left early.

Zlavik had first met Ollie Stevenson at my twenty-sixth birthday party. Ollie was drawn to Zlavik's jokes and wit. At that time Ollie's stuttering was getting worse, every fourth or fifth sentence was a sticky one.

Zlavik discovered Ollie was ready to buy a new car and offered to help. Ollie called me the next night to fill me in. "Jeeje-Je-sus, that guy is great. We spent all Saturday afternoon visiting five different dealers. We g-g-got a great deal."

After that, Ollie and Zlavik started hanging out, usually on Wednesday nights. Candlepin bowling became their specialty. Ollie found he was a natural. "After the second game I ne-ne-never went into the gutter again."

One Saturday afternoon, the three of us were all at Ollie's house having beer and pizza. "Ollie," Zlavik said gently. "I think I can help your stuttering. I know you feel bad about it."

"Wha-wha-what do you mean?"

"There is an energy thing I do with my hands. Let me try."

"This is some kind of jo-jo-joke, right?" Ollie was looking back and forth at both of us.

"No. I'll stand in back of you and put my hands on your temples for about three minutes. C'mon. What've you got to lose?"

"You're set-set-setting me up?" Ollie scrunched his face up even more and folded his arms. "I'm sensitive about my stu-stu-stuttering."

"Ollie," I said, "Zlavik got rid of my cold with his hands. Let him try."

Zlavik had Ollie continue to sit in the kitchen chair as he stood behind him. "Allen, get an ice cube. Ollie, I want you to put the ice cube in your mouth and focus on the cold. Nothing else."

Ollie, good Catholic that he was, took the ice cube as if it were a Holy Communion wafer. He closed his eyes and let his body slump as Zlavik's large hands touched either side of his head. Soon Zlavik's body shuddered as a corresponding tremor shot through Ollie. Another minute went by and Zlavik opened his eyes and removed his hands.

Ollie spat out the remainder of the ice cube. "What did you do? There was this intense heat and then this kind of electric shock thing."

Zlavik nodded and so did I.

"Jesus, I'm not stuttering! Jesus, I can't believe it! Hey, you changed something! You really did something! Jesus Christ!"

Zlavik nodded and sat down, looking embarrassed. "Look, guys, don't go blabbing about this. Okay? No big deal. I'm just some kind of conduit. Okay?"

We both nodded.

The next Saturday at Jackson's Restaurant, I told Zlavik that Ollie went the whole week without stuttering. His students couldn't get over it, and his parents were amazed. Ollie was telling people he went to a hypnotist as a cover story.

"Were you surprised it lasted?" Zlavik asked.

"I wasn't sure what to expect. What the hell did you do?"

"Keep your voice down." Zlavik frowned. "Intuitively, I get a hit that I can help, so I offer my services. The trick was to act, in the moment, on the feeling." His voice grew soft. "The source is outside of me. I don't understand it." He shrugged.

"I'd like to get you tested in a laboratory," I said.

"I don't do good work in laboratories. My gifts are shy." He winked.

When I got home that night, I told Thelma part of me believed Zlavik had a healing gift, but that part of me had doubts and thought it might be the placebo effect. Maybe Ollie had cured himself; I wasn't sure.

Thelma sat back with a smug look. "I've no doubt he has a healing gift. Frankly, I think you're envious of his range of talents. Everything flows from him: his warmth, his smile, his stride. Everything from you is forced. Your smile, your walk--even your laugh."

"Don't forget," I said, "that Prince Charming has a San Andreas Fault line gutting him down the middle."

"What do you mean?"

"His seizures. They're like two tectonic plates constantly rubbing together--twenty-four hours a day. He's on a collision course with himself." I was surprised at the loudness of my voice, but I added one final note. "And someday the whole thing will slide into the ocean."

Thelma's face tightened, signaling that Attila had arrived. "Your problem is that being with Zlavik is like being with Martin again. He outshines you in everything: physique, looks, personality--even intelligence. What good is that PhD of yours? Compared to him, you're a blocked showerhead. He's everything you're not."

"That's enough!"

"Look how people relate to him and love him. You're second fiddle to him just like you were to Martin. And part of you hates him--just like you hated Martin. Maybe you even want something bad to happen to him, too."

"That's bullshit!" I shouted, and without thinking, I slapped Thelma hard--with the back of my hand. I froze for a moment, shocked at what I'd done. Thelma stood still holding her cheek. I left the house--fast--and walked aimlessly for blocks. Part of me wanted to drive to Martin's grave but I resisted.

Three hours later, I returned to the house and apologized--four times. I even offered to see a counselor. Thelma remained silent the entire time. She was organizing her folders for her astrology class. I noticed a red mark on her right cheek. She slammed the door behind her.

I sat down in my chair and lit up a cigar. There was no one to whom I could confess my action. Atilla had hit the bullseye. I was angry with Zlavik. It was clear: everywhere I looked, there was imbalance. Zlavik's chronology didn't match; he bullshitted about things he didn't know. And he exaggerated; before he married Barbara at age twenty-two--if one believed him--he told me he had slept with over a hundred women, including two famous actresses. I loved him, but Thelma was right: part of me resented the hell out of him.

I dreamed that night of Martin and Zlavik. We were all young children playing on see-saws. Martin and I took the first turn. There was a gentle up-down rhythm to our play. Zlavik pushed Martin off and accelerated the rhythm in an erratic, wild manner. I cried and begged him to stop, but he wouldn't.

CHAPTER 16

I never told anyone about the slapping incident. And, to my surprise, Thelma told no one. In the weeks following, I let myself be distracted by a colleague of mine, Charlotte Stratton, an attractive, tall, willowy blonde who had a PhD in American Literature. About once a week, I would glance as Charlotte walked by my office and I would find myself yearning for a woman of her stability and quiet confidence.

Our classes were in the same building, and we saw each other often. She always had a smile and a friendly comment flecked with a wisp of a Georgia drawl. Fortunately, she was married and I kept my fantasies in check.

Thelma met Charlotte at a number of faculty parties and took an immediate dislike to her. She would mimic her mannerisms with an exaggerated accent. About once a month, Thelma would parade up and down the hallway using an open umbrella as a parasol to do her Charlotte imitation while making suggestive comments about "that nice Yankee boy, Allen Ford..." I continued to feign only platonic interest.

Charlotte and I evolved a routine of going out for coffee once a week. We both liked John Steinbeck and we discussed his books. During one coffee break, Charlotte jolted me with a blunt observation. "You and Thelma are so different--I'm surprised you're even together." I told her that my marriage to Thelma was due to an unknown past life crime of some notoriety. I laughed but could feel myself swallowing.

Soon Charlotte began to share her frustrations about her accountant husband Joe, an alcoholic. "I married for love and overlooked his fondness for the bottle." I continued to keep up a front about how things were with Thelma, but Charlotte always gave me a wry smile when I talked about my marriage.

On my return from a professional conference that summer, Thelma arranged a dramatic surprise for me. “Wait till you see what I’ve done!” She blindfolded me and led me up to the second floor. She was in her best Doris form, and I played along, as she led me into the small room by the bathroom.

“Holy shit!” I said, as she untied the blindfold.

The room had been transformed into a fully equipped baby’s room complete with changing table, crib, rocking chair, and bureau. The room was painted light blue, with white lacy curtains and a velveteen rabbit mobile over the crib. She kissed and hugged me nearly a dozen times.

“Didn’t I do a great job? I know it’ll be a boy.”

I went silent as I looked around the room. “I feel set-up,” I said in a firm voice.

Thelma shot me her darkest look. “Damn it! Quentin ran a special chart for me and said Jupiter is in the Fourth House--it’s the perfect time to get pregnant.” She pouted, pacing the room with her arms folded. “You don’t appreciate any of this. I worked twelve hours a day for three straight days!”

I left the room slamming the door behind me to the sounds of muffled curses.

I changed into my sweats and went for a six mile run. Later that evening, at bedtime, I slept--again--in the guest room. At breakfast, Thelma and I grunted a few words to each other as we prepared to go to work. Later, I called Zlavik and told him about the surprise nursery.

“Wow! She just threw it up overnight. Man, you’ve got your hands full.”

One day later, Thelma placed a lock on the room.

Zlavik got two promotions in the next two years at the Cabot Insurance Company. First, he was made the head of personnel--and he was only twenty-eight. “Man, I can’t believe how well I’m doing. My CEO invites me to hang out with him on Sundays. Boy, was he blown away when I fixed the manifold distribution cap on his classic 1938 Cadillac.”

“I know he gets a charge out of me,” he said, grinning. He added that his new promotion connected to the first of the three tasks. The proof was that he’d had only one seizure during the last year.

“So what’s this task?” I asked.

“Making my company one of the finest places to work in America.” He said there were two thousand employees working there and he was pushing for stock option purchases that would set the standard for the industry. In ten years the employees would own the company. Bruce was behind him, he said. Zlavik added that it could be a model for the whole country. "Plus I think this task leads to the second."

A wave of resentment moved through me as I looked at Zlavik. His clothes were impeccable--navy blue worsted wool slacks, light blue button down Oxford cloth shirt, a light grey wool v-neck sweater, and hundred dollar wine-colored tasseled loafers. I reflected on my friend's current assets: his marriage was more stable, his boss was mentoring him--and he was making twice my salary. Not bad for a guy with a GED. Thelma's comment about the dubious value of a PhD ricocheted back.

Just before Zlavik was ready to leave, I said, "It's been a year since I loaned you Sidney Hammond's book. What's your opinion of it?"

Zlavik's grin shifted into a tight look. "Look, I need to go." He got up and left without paying his bill.

My position at Chesterton University continued to be vexing. Dean Hammond was blocking me from teaching any new classes. He also plagued me with regular observations followed by scathing written evaluations. No one else in the entire Liberal Arts Department had received such visits. There were also ongoing rumors that my position might be eliminated by budget cutbacks.

My home life was still deteriorating. Thelma told me she'd lost interest in love-making. "Recreational sex, why should I bother--it will never lead to a baby."

She began sleeping in the guest bedroom and became even more involved in her astrology study group. She was out three nights a week. Almost every room in our house contained a pile of astrology books, magazines, journals and charts.

I occasionally drove the hour to Greenfield to see my mother and father. Dad was two years from retirement and had bought a twenty-eight foot sailboat that he was working on in the backyard. Conversations still didn't flow easily between us. I admitted to my parents that there were problems with my marriage. They weren't surprised.

"Is the counseling helping?" my mother asked.

"Well, Dr. Stevens sighs a lot when Thelma talks, and he suggested we look for another counselor."

My mother shook her head. "I'm sorry."

My father changed the subject to his sailboat. My parents always asked me about Zlavik whenever I visited. They'd met him a number of times and were taken with his charm. My mother seemed especially impressed. “He reminds me a lot of Martin...so buoyant, bright and optimistic and you seem so happy when you’re with him.” I nodded and looked away.

My mother followed me out to my car. She put both of her hands on my shoulders. “People expect too much from marriage--the real purpose is to survive.” She took her hands from my shoulder and kissed me on the forehead. I could feel a cold spot there all the way home.

In late November of 1978, the second of Zlavik’s three tasks materialized. Bruce Michaels took Zlavik out for an extended three-hour lunch at the Westbridge Country Club. Escargots began the meal, followed by poached salmon medallions topped off with banana flambé.

Zlavik called me later that evening. “You won’t believe what happened.” He sounded high.

“Cut to the chase.”

“I’ve been promoted to Director of Corporate Relations with a ten thousand dollar raise. That’s just the appetizer. Wait till you hear about the main dish.”

“So tell me!”

“Bruce wants me to run for the Sixth Congressional District seat in two years.” Michaels said he had the contacts and resources to get him the nomination. “I know this has got to be the second task.”

“Are you sure?”

“Absolutely,” he said. “It has to be, especially the way it builds on the first. And Bruce wants you involved because he knows we’re tight and he feels you have good judgement.”

“Sure,” I said. “What the hell. You could be great at this.” Inside I could feel my stomach tightening. I deserved a mentor like Bruce. I should have been the person Bruce wanted to support. I was the one that someday was going to fulfill Martin’s dream. And I was the one who had the passion and depth for our country and politics. Zlavik was illiterate on these subjects. I swallowed and listened.

The two of us met that following Saturday at Jackson’s Restaurant to go over Bruce’s plan. After an hour reviewing the document, I whistled. “Bruce has certainly lined up all the ducks.”

Zlavik explained how Bruce had analyzed the addresses of the two thousand employees at the company. Over fifteen hundred lived in the Sixth District. They’d be the core cadre of our organization. He looked up at me.

"Hey, Mr. Minister's son, am I going to have to sell my soul to do this?"

I took a long breath before answering. "This campaign can cut many ways." I hesitated. "The pressures will be on you and Barbara, and I worry how the stresses might affect your seizures." Zlavik flinched and I could see worry lines flash on his forehead.

"I haven't had a seizure for six months. Plus I'm in excellent shape. That's enough evidence for me." A smile re-ignited his face. "I'm certain this is the second task and that it will lead me to the last task. I'm finally getting focused on this mission. Right now I've got four years left." He looked at me directly. "This is the test of my life--and you're crucial to this election."

I wanted to say don't do it, but I pushed aside my reservations and my resentment.

"Do it," I said. "I'm in it with you, Mr. Congressman--up to my eye-balls!"

I found myself surprised by my spontaneity and emotion. Somehow I'd find a way to accept being Zlavik's second banana, we smiled and toasted with coffee cups.

"Damn, this is exciting." Zlavik's face was radiant. "Hey, how about being my Chief of Staff when I go to Washington?"

I laughed. "Let's concentrate on winning the primary, okay?"

Two weeks later, on a whim, I drove over to Zlavik's house. It was a humid Sunday afternoon and I needed a break from Thelma's complaining. Plus I knew Zlavik enjoyed unexpected drop-ins.

When I arrived at the house, Barbara said Zlavik was in the backyard removing an old stump. I walked around to the back and saw him: shirtless, his back facing me, swinging his axe at the base of the stump. I stayed still for a minute, not wanting to disturb his flow.

Trusting I could catch him during a break between swings, I moved closer. I moved closer still, then froze. There was a large X shaped scar on his back. I took three slow breaths.

In a clear, strong voice, I called to him by his old name: *"Rasputin."*

Zlavik dropped the axe and spun, arms and fists raised as in a fighting stance. His eyes were wide with alarm and his face, arm, and chest muscles were hyper-tensed. Upon seeing me his expression started to shift from alarm to relief.

"You saw the scar...huh. I've been wanting to tell you but I never knew quite how."

"Jesus Christ! I don't believe this!" I slapped the side of my head. "I've been dying to meet Rasputin for eleven years, and it turns out that he and my best friend are one and the same!"

Zlavik motioned me to lower my voice, pointing to the nearby houses.

We walked back to his house and sat down at the kitchen table, and Zlavik got out some lemonade. He waited for me to calm down, then explained why Rasputin had disappeared. He said David had confronted him during their last summer together about his role as a gang leader and the contradiction it represented to his uncle's teachings--Zlavik had agreed to drop it and move back to Seattle with his mother.

"No one ever knew my real identity, so I just disappeared."

I shook my head and laughed again at the discovery. "I always had this draw towards Rasputin that was almost--psychic. Now I got it. Man, does this shoot a hole through Sydney's book--wait till he finds out about it."

Zlavik made eye contact. "This thing could screw up my congressional bid--big time." I nodded. The shock had worn off and I realized the information could be damaging. Still, I remembered the night at the cocktail party where I taunted Sidney about Rasputin, unaware he was a few miles away.

One month after finding out about Zlavik's dual identity, I sat in on a meeting of the steering committee to elect Zlavik Johnson to the U.S. House of Representatives. Bruce Michaels opened the meeting in the mahogany paneled salon of the Westbridge Country Club. He explained that everyone present was selected with the objective of creating a cross-section of expertise to flesh-out the campaign's organization.

Michaels paused as he scanned the room to see the reaction of the fifty people present. "I am putting my energy, influence and contacts on the line because of an extraordinary young man who is destined for important roles. Zlavik, say a few words."

Zlavik stood up and beamed. "I'm here today from a deep sense of mission to be of service. I know this campaign is something I'm called to do."

I imagined myself in Zlavik's shoes, sighed, then let go and concentrated on taking extensive notes.

Two weeks later, Zlavik called and asked me to meet him at Jackson's Restaurant at four. "Something happened that I need to run by you." His voice was subdued.

After we got our coffee, Zlavik explained the news. He said that his cat, Palmer, was acting agitated around three in the morning. He found the cat in a window, back arched and hissing. "I looked out and saw that demon wolf. It's here now--in Connecticut."

"What does it mean?" I asked.

"I'm not sure. I first started to see it after I took a powerful hallucinogen that David gave me." He coughed. "Don't tell me I'm making it up--I know it's real."

During the next two years, Zlavik followed Bruce's strategic plan to the letter. He joined Kiwanis, Lions, and the Mason's. He was even attending church once a week with Barbara. "I feel like a hypocrite, but I've got to do it." His picture was in the papers regularly and I saw him frequently on the local news. Barbara seemed to be going along with it, but she was expressing doubts to Thelma. Zlavik had only one small seizure during this time, a sure sign from his view, that he was in alignment with the tasks. Overall, I never saw him more focused: his eyes were on the prize. And best of all, there were no more wolf sightings.

Thelma did a natal chart for Zlavik and said there were negative signs ahead, but I asked her to not say anything. Her specialty in astrology now was studying the influences of the North Node. I'd drive by her astrologer's house and fantasize heaving an oversize Molotov cocktail through his picture window--on a night with a full moon of course.

The rift between Thelma and me continued to widen. The baby room remained locked and the issue of children was still a forbidden topic. I saw less of Doris, and more of either Norma or Atilla. We'd taken a long break from seeing our marriage counselor--at Thelma's insistence. Our growing involvement in Zlavik's campaign, along with our jobs, kept us busy. We continued to live the charade of being two polite, distant roommates.

The campaign fed me as I began working sixteen hour days, teaching during the day and working nights and weekends on the campaign. Both Bruce and Zlavik asked me to be the chairman, which I accepted. I reminded myself that, somehow, Martin's spirit was in Zlavik and the run for office was helping fulfill the original dream.

However, during lulls in the schedule, I could still feel pulls to work things out with Thelma. On impulse, I persuaded her to resume our counseling. We'd had three more sessions before Dr. Stevens lost his cool after one of Thelma's outbursts. "You are the angriest woman I've ever met and I can no longer work with you." Thelma demanded to know his birth date but Stevens refused. Thelma left the session and I followed her to the car.

At dinner that night I spilled vinaigrette salad dressing on Thelma's favorite lace linen tablecloth. Attila bolted out of her cave. "Fucking idiot--you can't do anything right!" She grabbed the salad dressing bottle and emptied the rest of the contents beside her plate. "We might as well have stereo stains."

Something snapped in me. I started pounding the table with my fists.

"No! No! No!"

I kept up the refrain, my voice getting louder and louder as I continued pounding. Thelma covered her ears.

"No! No! No!"

Attila slumped away. Norma appeared. "You've never loved me. Deep down, I never felt it was there."

I pounded the table again, causing her favorite crystal glass to smash to the floor. "Once and for all, what do you need for proof?"

She covered her face with both hands. She began sobbing. Garbled words came out between sobs: "How can I believe you love me when I don't love myself."

I got quiet. There was nothing to say, do or think.

After that fight, I knew I wanted to see more of Charlotte. She and Joe were in the process of separating. We began to go out for coffee several-times a week and gave each other support--she now knew the truth about my marriage. We sensed the mutual pull but skirted discussions about it.

CHAPTER 17

In September of 1980, Zlavik was at the Westbridge Hotel Ballroom holding his official press conference, announcing his candidacy. I'd come up with the idea of having two hundred volunteers from the district stand behind him as he gave the speech I'd written.

The local media turnout was excellent and included newspaper, radio, and cable, plus a Hartford TV station. Zlavik wore a pin-striped navy blue suit, a red striped tie and pale blue oxford shirt. He stressed the theme of citizen participation. As he answered questions, his demeanor was an adroit combination of humor and seriousness, and his smile was bright and winning.

He grabbed me when he stepped away from the podium and whispered. "Two tasks down, one to go."

I was pleased with my role as campaign manager. My responsibilities were the day to day operations as well as the formulation of our policy positions. I could feel the cord with Martin re-surfacing.

During the press conference I focused on one face—Ian MacDonald, the chief political writer for the *Westbridge Herald.* A first cousin of Sydney Hammond, he was about five feet eight inches tall, and except for his full head of hair, a Groucho Marx look alike with his brown horn-rimmed glasses and large mustache. His suits were always rumpled and sprinkled with grey ash flecks from his ever-present cigarette. Despite his careless exterior, Ian MacDonald was well known for his caustic but polished writings. MacDonald wielded power and influence from his weekly column called, *Inside the County.*

He sneered throughout the press conference and took no notes. He knew I'd been a campaigner for McGovern, and I nodded to him as I passed by.

"Oh, I see the preppie-do-gooder has found another white horse to ride."

I smiled, saying nothing, but he stopped me.

"Come on Ford, how can you back such a lightweight?"

"Don't underestimate Zlavik," I said. "He could bring large numbers of new people into the political process."

"I can't buy it. He's a pretty boy, who's being orchestrated by Bruce Michaels. Hell, everybody says Bruce is using Zlavik as a surrogate for his dead son."

The following Sunday, Ian MacDonald's column appeared:

Zlavik the Slick

Zlavik Johnson, age 31, of Southampton, has officially announced his candidacy for the U.S. House of Representatives. He stated that the theme of his campaign was one of extensive citizen involvement in all phases of government.

In this columnist's opinion, he is one of the least qualified candidates to run for higher office I have ever seen. Johnson stated that he wanted to see a citizens' crusade on Washington. Historians tell us the four Crusades to free the Holy Land were all disasters. I predict the same fate for those who try to follow "Zlavik the Slick" to the holy land.

Zlavik phoned me that night. "I can't believe MacDonald can be allowed to write that stuff."

"You've got to expect criticism like this--it's normal. This column was mild compared to others I've read."

Zlavik groaned. I was surprised at his naivete.

It was in July that the first internal problem appeared in the campaign. Her name was Alana Colby. She was twenty-one, red hair, bright and as vivacious as she was voluptuous. And as Ollie Stephenson observed, "she was built like the ultimate brick shit-house." Alana spent all her spare time at the main campaign office.

It took me more time than others to notice the long, lingering looks between Zlavik and Alana. I picked up the scent of what was going on when I noticed Zlavik starting to give Alana rides home. I wasn't surprised when I heard rumors of an affair. I held off for a month before I confronted Zlavik in an early morning meeting at Jackson's.

"No bullshit. Are you having an affair with Alana?"

Zlavik was calm. "Yes."

"The timing is terrible." I threw him a look of disgust.

"Allen, hear me out...she came on to me...I rebuffed her three times before I consented. She knows it's short-lived. Damn it! I've been faithful to Barbara for seven years. This is the only time I..."

I interrupted. "You don't get it. Shit like this can gut everything."

Zlavik grabbed my left arm hard, till it hurt. "Listen carefully." He paused, apologized, and let go of my arm. "This affair is giving me something I haven't had in a long time. The sexual energy is extraordinary...somehow it's helping me get to the third task. Crazy, huh?"

"Yeah, real crazy."

We talked more and both of us cooled down. He agreed to wind down the affair. "I think it was coming to a close anyway." I was relieved.

I discovered that our major opponent in the general election in November, would be, to both my dismay and pleasure, Dean Sydney Hammond III. His wife, Andrea, was using her family wealth to bankroll his campaign. I knew this would create more tension at work, but I didn't care. Zlavik thought it was funny. "Even if I lose, I'll get you a job at my company." He laughed again observing that my next evaluation would likely be a corker.

We had one serious opponent in the Democratic Primary, Howard Rich, a five term state representative. He was well financed, respected--and dull. All parties agreed that there would only be one debate for the primary election. Zlavik took four days off to prime himself on the issues.

The first debate went well until the last ten minutes when the three candidates had the opportunity to question each other. What no one knew was Charlie Madden, our local perennial candidate--for everything--had a bomb to deliver in the form of a photograph. The explosive device was set to detonate in minutes--after asking a few setup questions. Charlie held up a large manila envelope in both hands as he turned to Zlavik.

"Mr. Johnson, do you feel the voters deserve high ethical standards?"

"Of course."

"What do you think about a candidate who commits adultery?"

Our group went stone silent.

Zlavik's eyes got big, but he was otherwise keeping his cool. "I fail to see your point."

Madden enjoyed the moment as he slowly withdrew the glossy, large photograph which the camera zoomed in on for a close-up. There was

Zlavik in a passionate embrace with Alana. "Mr. Johnson is having an affair with a young college volunteer. He's an adulterer and a phony."

A dozen of us were at Bruce's house following the debate on TV. A collective silence took over the room. Bruce leaned over to me and whispered, "What the hell is this about?"

I swallowed. "This is a bunch of crap--the photo has been doctored." I was surprised how easily I lied. There continued to be heavy silence in the room for another minute. Thelma moved closer and put her arm around Barbara's shoulder who was sitting there sullen and flushed.

We looked at the screen to see Zlavik still appearing relaxed. "I know I don't have to respond, but I'd like to answer."

After hesitation, the moderator nodded. "You have one minute."

Zlavik looked directly into the camera, not to Madden. "I've done nothing wrong with any volunteer on my campaign. Any photograph can be taken out of context, or distorted. My conscience is clear."

Ollie grabbed my arm and whispered, "How the hell does he stay so calm?"

I sighed. "He's one of a kind."

Cheering broke out in the room. Zlavik had recovered.

I rushed home and phoned Alana Colby, who answered in a quavering voice. "I'm scared, I don't want to ruin Zlavik's chance of winning. What should I do?"

I'd planned out what I'd say. "Is there a friend or relative, in another part of the country, you could visit until the hubbub dies down?"

"Yes, I have relatives in Sacramento."

"Good. Get a ticket and leave tomorrow. Don't talk to anyone." I told her the campaign would reimburse her. I then called Zlavik at home and told him what I'd done. He hesitated, then grunted his approval.

"How did you keep your cool when Charlie whipped out that photo?"

"In my heart I didn't believe we'd done anything wrong. We're two consenting adults. What we shared helped each of us."

"This could still screw up the entire campaign. I covered for you with Bruce, but I'm pissed."

The next morning I organized a damage control meeting at the headquarters. We all agreed that our cover story would be that the photo was doctored. Several newspapers called saying they had gotten the photo sent to them--anonymously. I registered a quick shudder, as I became aware I was repeating the cover story, knowing it was a lie. Fortunately, all the papers agreed not to print it. "Who knows," I said to myself, "maybe Sydney Hammond was behind the whole thing." Perhaps he had a mole inside our campaign. Then again, perhaps Zlavik's risky behavior was the real culprit.

For the first time, I found myself doubting his suitability as a Congressman. Several times a day there was a stirring in my gut as the thought came back that I should be in Zlavik's shoes, or that if Martin were alive he would be the candidate. Plus, I was tired of how Zlavik linked every quirk from his affair, to his seizures, to his crazy uncle, to the reality of the three tasks. What if it was all a made-up fable that Zlavik's psyche rigged up for some convoluted purpose? Perhaps I was a dupe following the emperor who had no clothes.

Zlavik came by my house later that evening. He apologized for the affair saying he was wrong and he reiterated how important I was to him and the campaign. He said there would be no other screw ups. I told him about the upset caused by my father's affair and its effect on me. He nodded, saying he understood now, how innocent parties could get hurt. He repeated again how the campaign was at the core of accomplishing the three tasks. We laughed and joked about all that had happened so far in our friendship.

I was committing again to Zlavik's campaign as a vehicle to fulfill Martin's dream. This was my special task, I reasoned. We gave each other a long bear hug before he left. I had my new brother back and I wasn't going to lose this one.

Later that night, I dreamed that it was Martin who was running for Congress. The crowds were bigger and the endorsements were flowing. And there were no glitches or doubts in my gut. Martin and I were together everywhere doing everything. President Kennedy showed up at the last rally and stood between the two of us holding up both our hands.

"Those Ford Brothers are something else!" The crowd cheered wildly.

CHAPTER 18

I'd arranged for the campaign to kick into high gear during July with over three hundred active volunteers. Zlavik attended over two hundred "coffees" that summer to make extensive personal contact with undecided voters. Our goal was victory over our opponent, Howard Rich, by a double digit.

I still had occasional fantasies about being the candidate. However, I would remind myself that, somehow, Zlavik was Martin's replacement and I was fulfilling my mission by being number two.

In August, another campaign weakness surfaced. Ollie took me aside to tell me. "Do you ever notice how Zlavik plays with the truth? He has this way of making up things." Ollie had a scowl on his face and his arms were folded across his chest.

"What happened?" I asked.

Ollie described a recent meeting at the Westbridge Senior Citizen's Center. Zlavik was asked a question about possible Medicare coverage for drug prescriptions. He didn't skip a beat, smiling his big smile and stating there was a house sub-committee working on the issue. "There were eighty-five people present." Ollie was shocked.

Zlavik had lied to a large group of people, and his response, when confronted, was to say, "In the long run does it really matter? C'mon, you're taking everything too seriously." This was followed by a hearty laugh and a whack on the back. I told Ollie I would talk to Zlavik, however, most things were going well and I kept putting the issue off.

In late August I met with Bruce Michaels for lunch to brief him on campaign business. I always felt intimidated by Michaels' large six foot, six inch frame, his two PhD's, and his career as Undersecretary of Commerce in the Johnson Administration. It was halfway through lunch when he said, "After two terms as a Congressman, Zlavik should go for a U.S. Senate seat, which would give him a total of ten years in elective office."

Bruce told me he was sixty-two years old and soon to retire. He was planning to devote the next ten years of his life preparing Zlavik for the national stage. He added that he'd numerous important political and financial contacts throughout the country. "All of this will be focused on the cause."

"What are you getting at?"

"Zlavik should go for the presidency." Michaels leaned back in his chair. "No one comes close to possessing Zlavik's gifts. The image he could project on TV of warmth, confidence, and intelligence would be unparalleled."

Michaels added that he saw a rare emerging moment in human history. "Maybe once every thousand years a juncture of possibilities like this occurs." The computer, he believed, would be the catalyst that would usher the world into a new Golden Era, where abundance and peace could be created on a scale never before imagined. "I see him potentially, as a giant figure in world history."

Bruce fixed me with his gaze. "I know I can make this happen." He pounded the table with his right fist, rattling all the dishes.

I was dazed from the grandiosity of his vision, although I recalled Uncle David's prediction that Zlavik could be an important leader. It took me several moments to respond. "My God...Bruce...I don't know what to say."

"I know you're thinking about his seizures, but look what FDR accomplished from a wheelchair. And look at all the health problems Jack Kennedy overcame. I know Zlavik's educational credentials are weak, but all Truman had was a high school degree."

"This is all very new," I said in a subdued voice.

"I want you to be aware of this plan." He leaned over and spoke in a low voice. "I see you as his Chief of Staff at the White House. You two have a remarkable rapport--you could be the penultimate team to go down in the history books."

I smiled and took a long drink from my shaking water glass. Bruce paid the bill and signaled me the meeting was over. I wrestled with Bruce's vision. I was both dazed and awed. I had to run the scenario by someone or go on a drinking binge, so before I left the country club, I called Ollie.

"I need to see you," I told him. It's urgent."

The Cellar was a college beer and pizza joint that was deserted at three in the afternoon. Ollie arrived there five minutes after I did.

"Ford, you look wired--what's up?"

"You won't believe this." I scanned the nearby tables.

"Shoot."

After ten minutes, Ollie knew the story. He was silent for a long while, he rubbed his jaw. "Zlavik in the White House? Anther FDR? Well, we'd upgrade our parties, that's for sure." He laughed, and so did I.

After a long swallow of beer, Ollie grabbed three pretzels and launched into his own White House fantasy. First he'd ask for the job of Secretary of State. He paused, then smiled. "My father would finally be proud of his ex-stuttering son--the shortest Secretary of State ever. My place in history would be assured."

"But how would Zlavik fare as President?" I asked.

"The press corp will be fascinated with his charm and wit until someone catches him screwing some maid in a closet, like Harding did. Then there would be a huge budget deficit because Zlavik hates saying no."

"Next," I added, "Mike Wallace would interview Alana Colby on *Sixty Minutes*." I frowned, shook my head and took a long drink from my beer.

Ollie had his hand up. His expression softened. "You know, he does have the personality and brains that high office requires, but he is too sweet a guy." Before we left, I swore Ollie to secrecy.

At dinner that evening I told Thelma about the conversation with Bruce. The campaign continued to be the excuse to put off a divorce as we worked our sixteen hour days. I'd assigned Thelma to a small office ten miles away to avoid any friction; two of the volunteers there were astrology buffs, and I knew Thelma would be entranced.

Something shifted as we did dishes together after supper. Doris was back for an overnight. She put on soft music and asked me to dance. We each had a second glass of wine, and the warm feelings began circling and swirling us back to the highs of our first year. Doris cooed to me as we danced, telling me how much she loved me. I was feeling passion again because I knew the wine was keeping Norma and Atilla locked-up.

Then we were in the bedroom. The magic of Bermuda resurrected in full bloom. We made love--twice. When we finished Thelma broke down and sobbed. She said, "I've put you through eleven years of hell--I'm so sorry."

I said nothing, letting her hold on tight as she fell asleep. I gazed at her face in her slumber. I gave her a light kiss on the forehead and felt like I was saying good-bye.

At seven the next morning, I was awakened with a call from Zlavik. "Allen, I need to talk."

"What's up?"

"I saw the wolf again last night in the backyard; it was illuminated by the moonlight, just sitting looking up." He said he'd not slept the rest of the night.

"Did you try to take photos of the wolf or its tracks?"

"Look, I've told you before, the thing is from another dimension--it wouldn't show up. You've got to stay open on this. You're the only one I'm sharing this with."

"Sure, okay," I muttered as I hung up.

CHAPTER 19

On the night of the primary four hundred people turned out for our victory party at the Westbridge Hotel Ballroom. The crowd sang and snake-danced through the hallways till early morning. A number of people congratulated me on my work as chairman. Bruce took me aside and said my quota system for each precinct had worked beautifully. I was buoyant. Martin's vision was on track.

Within a week of the primary win, new and unexpected problems emerged. First, pressure was coming from Sydney Hammond for us to prove that Zlavik had a GED. We saw it as a ploy and ignored the demand; however, Zlavik avoided eye contact whenever I brought up the issue. I had a queasy feeling, but I pushed it aside.

Our Steering Committee met and reviewed the strategic plan for the remaining six weeks of the campaign. We realized Hammond was a formidable candidate. He was getting a stream of money, as well as help from the national party. Also, he had contacts left over from his grandfather who had been a prominent U.S. Senator.

We also heard ongoing rumors that Ian MacDonald was planning a surprise for us. The gift appeared in the form of a featured story on the front page of the *Sunday Westbridge Herald.* Somehow Ian had been tipped off about the Rasputin connection. MacDonald had utilized Hammond's book extensively, but cited only the worst activities of Rasputin. The lead story read as if Zlavik's youth placed him in the FBI top ten category.

Additionally, MacDonald had interviewed Zlavik's mother, stepfather, and other relatives and caught other discrepancies. First, he never obtained a GED. Second, he never attended a local community college as he had claimed. Third, he had been in the service for only six months, not two years. Zlavik's mother, in a fit of incredible naivete, also told MacDonald that Zlavik had been on probation when he was fourteen.

I was thrown because only five people knew of his past as Rasputin. Zlavik himself, me, Thelma, Barbara, and Ollie. All were loyal to Zlavik. I considered Thelma as a possible mole, but she loved Zlavik as much as I did; there was no motivation for her to do such a thing.

I called Zlavik immediately. Barbara answered the phone. "He broke down this morning when he saw the paper. He told me the campaign is over." Barbara said Zlavik wanted a press conference for nine Monday morning."

"Are you certain? If he no-shows, it'll be the final blow."

"I'm positive."

I received a call from Zlavik around nine that night. He was ready to withdraw, but wanted my advice. I urged him to stay. We talked for several hours about ideas and strategies that he could use in the press conference. I kept repeating the idea of turning his checkered background into an asset. "Zlavik," I said, "it's your best card--play it."

Zlavik walked through the doors of our headquarters at exactly eight fifty-nine Monday morning. There were over sixty people there, including radio, television, and numerous newspaper personnel as well as a core group of supporters. Even the *New York Times* had sent a reporter. Ian MacDonald stood in the center of the press with a smirk on his face.

Zlavik was dressed in a light blue, short sleeve polo shirt with dark grey dress slacks; he looked neat--with the exception of his unshaven face. He was subdued as he sat in front of the bank of microphones at the table. He had no notes with him.

Zlavik nodded okay to the media and staff. "I've called this press conference to respond to a story in Sunday's *Westbridge Herald*. First, Ian, let me congratulate you." All eyes shifted to Ian, who looked away and scowled. "You did everyone a favor by printing this story. Your facts are correct."

Then Zlavik admitted he was the gang leader Rasputin. He shared how he moved to Seattle, with his mother, as a way to start a new life. He admitted that everything about him was now open to doubt, and that he had made some serious mistakes. "Right now I want to apologize to all my supporters and to the public."

He said he'd been reading a lot of American history books in the last year. "The American experiment," he said, "has always defied the odds."

He paused. "I feel that way about my experiment. I've wrestled whether to drop out. Right now, I know I'm a long shot, but I deeply believe in my ability--and mission--to make things happen. I believe this is the most important thing I've ever done." He sighed and made eye contact with me.

I gave him a big thumbs up and grinned. Zlavik refocused and said he'd leave the decision to stay or quit based on postcards sent to him by voters in the district. "And I'm telling you," he said, "I'll do things for the district that Sydney Hammond can only dream of."

Zlavik then opened Hammond's book and read the well-known description of him. "Perhaps one in a hundred thousand have the constellation of genes..." He closed the book. "My opponent, a brilliant scholar, has validated my credentials for this office beyond any endorsement I've yet received."

All the volunteers, staff, Bruce, Ollie and myself were on our feet applauding and shouting. Even a few reporters were clapping. Ian MacDonald was red-faced and glaring.

Only one reporter caught the import of the Rasputin story, Mark Roper of the *New York Times*. He was familiar with Sydney's book. One week later, he did a feature story on the irony of a brilliant academic vying for a congressional seat against a former gang leader whom he once insisted was either doomed or dead.

He entitled the story, "Rasputin vs. the Dean." In a play on Hammond's quote, Roper said, "It would seem that the genes of Zlavik Johnson may indeed overcome the privileged environment of Sydney Hammond." The story was picked up by our local papers and given wide play.

Also helping us was the strategy I told Zlavik to follow by going on the offensive and having a whirlwind of radio and TV interviews. He was everywhere, beaming his expansive smile, admitting his mistakes and asking for a second chance. The vote results were impressive. Out of six thousand postcards received, five thousand said "Stay." The underdog had become the top dog.

I resumed my weekly coffee meetings with Charlotte, who was now officially divorced. She praised Zlavik for his recovery at the press conference, and she shared that people were noticing my work as campaign chair. "People are saying you're the brains behind everything." She grabbed both my hands and said, "By the way, there are feelings here for you when you're ready." I smiled and held her hands until it was time to leave.

With one month left in the campaign, Zlavik and Hammond were in a dead heat. However, ten percent of the voters were undecided. Once again, I saw a crisis galvanize our cadre of workers. After Zlavik's press conference, we had a few people quit, but the rest had taken Zlavik even further into their hearts.

During that time period I received a letter from the President of Chesterton University stating that my position was being eliminated at the end of the academic year due to budgetary cutbacks. My sources told me it was Sydney's payback; he had manipulated the budget in order to jettison me.

The letter depressed me, but I reminded myself that I had a fifty-fifty shot at being Zlavik's Chief of Staff--and we could become a team that would make a difference in Washington. I slumped back in my chair in the den and picked up Martin's picture from the desk.

CHAPTER 20

The last two weeks of the campaign saw Zlavik campaigning eighteen hours a day, seven days a week. Everywhere we went people were coming up and wishing him well.

"Oh, Mr. Johnson, can I have your autograph? I just know, someday, you're going to be famous," said a high school girl at a shopping mall rally.

"Damn, it's like being a movie star," he said, grinning in an aside to me as he signed the autograph. "It'll be close, but we'll pull it off. I know this is the most important of the three tasks. If I win, the third one will fall into place." I watched him go back into the crowd and feed off their energy like a suckling pig.

I continued to be pleased with what I'd done in my role as campaign chair. Every precinct was organized, and had a quota of votes to achieve. We were door-to-door canvassing on a level never done before. And we had the largest volunteer staff ever seen in a congressional race. The *Westbridge Herald* did a feature story on my role as campaign chair, stressing my innovative techniques, and best of all, my work felt imbued more than ever with Martin's spirit.

Ten days before the election, the polls were showing contradictory results. The *Westbridge Herald* had Hammond and Zlavik in a dead heat. Our own poll showed us winning by a five percent margin, but a local TV station had Hammond winning by four.

One week before the election the Hammond campaign unleashed two chilling television ads that were shown dozens of times daily. The first showed Zlavik at the press conference where he admitted lying. However, all the explanations were cut-off. "I lied about my education...I lied about my military service...I lied about my job history." The second came two days later and began with a small photo of the embrace between Alana and Zlavik. There was no commentary. All you heard was Zlavik's quote from the debate: "I've done nothing wrong." The photo became larger and larger as the refrain-- "I've done nothing wrong" grew louder and louder.

"Get the ad off the TV--it's killing us." All our precinct workers were calling me with the same message. I asked Bruce Michaels to pressure both TV stations, but neither station gave into his pleadings or threats. We countered with press releases, but the effect was minimal. Our campaign workers grew more upset. Thelma cried whenever either ad came on.

On the fourth day of the negative ad barrage, Barbara called. "Zlavik had a thirty minute seizure this morning--it was the worst I've seen in three years--cancel everything for the next two days." We covered by saying he was in strategy sessions.

On election day the following Tuesday, a subdued crowd of two hundred supporters awaited the election results at the Westbridge Hotel Ballroom. By eight p.m., the trend was clear: we were losing in almost every precinct.

At nine, Zlavik came down from his hotel room and received strong applause from the crowd, who chanted his name. He strode to the podium smiling and waving. "I've got good news and bad news." The crowd grew silent. "The good news is you've been the finest political organization ever seen in this state. You've been incredible! The bad news is those negative ads reversed our work. I am conceding the election to Sydney Hammond."

The crowd groaned, and Zlavik raised his hand to silence them. He then waded out in the crowd to thank people, working his way to the main exit doors where he stationed himself. He either touched, kissed or hugged every person who was in the room. The ballroom was empty by eleven, and Zlavik was leaning against the door, distant and drained.

Tradition required we go to Hammond's headquarters--where their victory party was still taking place and congratulate him. We entered through the main doors and Hammond's crowd spotted us and quieted. Zlavik went to the front of the room and shook Sydney's hand and those of his family members. Then he went to the podium.

"I congratulate Sydney on his election. We both worked hard and offered the voters a clear choice. And I honor the greater process we're all part of."

A Hammond supporter leaned towards me. "Your guy is a class act--part of me wanted to vote for him."

"I wish I could say the same for our new Congressman." The man glared and walked away.

Sydney signaled me to come over. “Sorry about your position being cut next year, and now it looks like you won’t have a job in Washington either.” He smirked and my stomach locked up as my fists tightened. “Oh,” he added, “do thank your lovely wife for all her help.”

Zlavik and I returned to the private suite at the Westbridge Hotel that we had reserved for the Steering Committee. About a half dozen people remained there. Bruce Michaels had not bothered to show. Ollie said he had been downing scotches in the bar downstairs. By one, everyone had left, except Zlavik and me. Zlavik locked the door.

“Damn!” he said. I worked my ass off, seven days a week for two years for that seat. The thing had my name on it for Christ’s sake!” He kicked the door hard. “And that fucking photo appears...the hug was four seconds long--yet it destroyed two years of work. What happened isn’t right!”

Soon he was shaking and crying. “I’m so angry with myself...” His hands covered his face, and he sat down. “This election was supposed to be the second of the three tasks. Hell, it was supposed to lead to the third. I don’t know where I am now.” He took a long breath. “I question everything.”

The words came out of me in a quiet voice. “Let the loss go.”

“Easy for you to say,” he snapped. “You don’t face the reality of a year to live, which is compounded by the fact that I just blew the second task; now my stepping stone to the third task is gone. I feel like I got hurled back to the starting gate. So much for my seven year quest.”

He sat back in the sofa. “Allen, you should’ve been the congressional nominee. You’ve got the educational credentials, profession, and clean personal life.” He sighed and looked at me.

“Yeah, but you forgot one thing.” Zlavik raised his eyebrows. “No way is Washington ready for ‘Zodiac Zoe.’”

He laughed and said, “Let’s get out of here.” As I drove him home he was silent except for the drumming of his fingers on the dashboard. We both got out of the car and looked up at the full moon. He put his arms on my shoulders and hugged me. Then he cupped his hands around his mouth and howled at the moon, waved, and laughed as if everything had washed over him.

I drove home while Sydney’s comment about Thelma played back to me. If my wife were in fact, the mole, her actions sank Zlavik’s candidacy more than any other element. Then, again, was Sydney just setting me up? Numbness returned in my chest as I pulled into my driveway. I stayed in the car for a long time.

CHAPTER 21

Thelma and I awoke late. After breakfast, I went out and did yard work all day. At dinner I asked the question. "Did you leak information to Hammond's campaign?"

She stiffened and said, "I'd never pass on confidential information."

I remained suspicious remembering her disclosure to Andrea Hammond about Martin's death. Thelma was quiet as she picked at her chicken cordon bleu. She drank two glasses of wine with her meal and began sending me non-stop piercing looks.

"What's going on?" I asked.

"I'm giving you one last chance."

"For what?"

"I want to get pregnant."

I spilled my wine. "That's bullshit."

Doris assumed a calm matter-of-fact manner.

"Okay. I want a divorce then...I'm clear now."

I was thrown. This wasn't Attila or Norma but a self-assured Doris who knew what she wanted. At the end of the week, I gave in to the steady drumbeat of Doris' doubts and agreed to a divorce.

The night before she left, she had a smile on her face. "Quentin Burrows," she said, "my astrology teacher, has been my lover for the last six months. I'm going to move in with him."

"Why the hell did you bring up the baby thing again?"

She frowned. "I was willing to give our relationship one more chance."

"What kind of logic is that?" I pushed away from the table. "Actually, the question now is whether Zodiac Zoe can find Camelot on the North Node."

I could see her eyes scouring for a water glass, but I left for an eight mile jog. On Monday, when I came home from work, I found that Thelma had moved out taking all her clothes, her three teddy bears and her favorite pictures. For some reason I felt peaceful in the somewhat empty house.

Zlavik dropped by in the weeks that followed my separation. We talked about everything that had happened in our seven years together. In our new round of conversations Zlavik said he was exploring the idea that the campaign was still the second task, except the purpose had been to bring hundreds of people into the political process. "Our campaign stirred people up." He leaned back, flashing his most expansive smile.

After a few moments of silence my friend said, "A couple of times I played with the idea that our friendship might be the third task." He said it fulfilled the criteria of an outstanding accomplishment plus I was a linchpin for both his job and the campaign. "If you are the third, then maybe I, in fact, have arrived."

I was both embarrassed and honored. And I too, wondered if our friendship was the third task. Why not? The relationship had grown for seven years and felt deep and rich. Maybe Zlavik's mission was complete.

One month after Thelma moved in with Quentin, I got a late night call from Westbridge's leading astrologer. Thelma had just overturned his fifty gallon aquarium on him; she was now outside drenching him through an open window with a garden hose.

"What do I do?" he asked. "What do I do?"

"Review her natal chart!" I slammed down the phone.

In my unfolding new life, one of the hallmarks continued to be my weekly meetings with Zlavik, every Saturday afternoon at our corner booth at Jackson's Restaurant. He still loved to write on napkins and project business ideas. However, over time, he spoke less of the three tasks. If I raised the issue he would crack a joke and change the topic. He was very happy when I gave him the news that Winston Northrup said my job was reinstated now that Hammond had left.

During this time, Zlavik spent more time at the archery range. He'd go there both Saturday and Sunday mornings. One day in late May, I went looking for him. He wasn't at his usual spot. I knew he had a habit of going off to the nearby woods and meditating by a secluded pond, so I walked down a pine needle encrusted path to the pond looking for him.

An early morning mist hung over the water, and I sat on a rock enjoying the sweetness of the smell from some nearby honeysuckle. Then I saw a flash of red through some brush. I moved in closer and saw Zlavik beside a fallen tree trunk, crouched on the ground on all fours growling and laughing. The haze cleared, and I saw the object of his attention: a small, red fox pup. They were having a mock fight. The pup growled; Zlavik growled. The pup pawed the dirt; Zlavik pawed the dirt. He was in one continuous fluid flow mirroring the pup: action by action, move by move.

Then Zlavik grabbed a foot-long twig and placed it in his mouth, straight out, taunting the fox. The pup grabbed hold, and a tug of war ensued. Back and forth went the twosome, growling happily for control.

The stick snapped, with the pup getting the larger portion. Zlavik spit out his piece and laughed, "Well, my feisty friend, you won." The pup circled Zlavik as if reveling in its victory. Zlavik laughed again, "Show off!"

Then I noticed a large red fox walking along the pond's edge towards a clearing, about a hundred yards away. "Zlavik," I said. The mother fox is coming. You'd better leave."

Startled, Zlavik stood up. He spotted the mother, pivoted, and headed through the brush toward my voice, his face flushed.

"I hope you don't think I was immature. Damn, we were having fun."

"You were great. I'd give anything to play like that."

In June of 1983, six months after moving out, our divorce was finalized. Thelma had left Quentin after their water fight, and was now living in New York City. Things were relatively calm between us, and I told her that I'd take her out after the hearing to her favorite Chinese restaurant. She ordered her preferred meal of Moo-Goo-Gai-Pan, and looked at me across the table.

"I never wanted this divorce--I was testing you. The thing with Quentin was part of the plan. I wanted you to put your foot down and say no, but you never did."

I stood quickly, put on my jacket and, in one seamless move, emptied the pitcher of water, ice cubes and all, over her. I left without paying the bill. I felt a rush of cool August air as I walked out to the street

After eight months of being seizure free, Zlavik had a serious seizure at work. He was out the rest of the week. A month later, he had a second seizure while at Ollie's house, and during his thrashing, he knocked over Ollie's entertainment center, damaging his TV and stereo system.

I was worried. Zlavik now said little about the three tasks, but the giant wolf was showing up more often. He'd always call me after a sighting, which was usually at night and signaled by Palmer, his cat, who would wake him. I noticed a new edgy quality in his voice.

Zlavik reminded me that there was only one year left according to the original message. "Increased seizures are the signal that I failed," he added. Another concern was the increasing coldness from Bruce Michaels. "Bruce had a plan for me--I screwed up big time. He's still bullshit."

Without Thelma, Ollie became my main sounding board about Zlavik. He knew all the details of the three tasks, the wolf, and just about anything else connected to our mutual friend.

Ollie munched more pretzels and ate faster whenever he talked about Zlavik's plight. "Look, either he's hooked up to a spiritual conduit most of us can't grasp, or he's manufactured himself one hell of an ingenious death sentence." Ollie shook his head. "Go figure."

I told Ollie that I felt Zlavik had a genuine connection to a spiritual source but I wasn't sure about the three tasks. I was confused--and the wolf business really threw me.

Ollie added one postscript. He'd gotten a book out from the college library about wolves. "Wolves aren't solitary--they live only in groups. Plus there is no record of a wolf killing a man in the North American continent." He added that a wolf hadn't been spotted in our state for a hundred years, and that the only giant wolf mentioned lived in the Pleistocene Era--fifty-million years ago.

"The wolf comes from another dimension, that's why it's not in the books." Ollie blanched at my comment. I hesitated, then added. "I don't know where the truth ends and fantasy begins."

Thelma gave me yet one more parting gift in the form of a letter sent to me three months after our divorce. She had started therapy and said she had to clear her conscience with yet one more confession. Lydia Hammond, Sydney's cousin, had been in her astrology class for the last two years. Thelma admitted leaking a number of confidences including the Alana Colby affair, and even the Rasputin story. "I played a game with myself, believing that Lydia would keep my confidences."

After reading the letter, I had four beers before I called Ollie and told him what she'd written. Thelma Menninger Ford, with her careless prattle had, single handedly, sunk Zlavik's campaign, his second task, Martin's dream, and two years of the hardest work of my life. I looked for a picture of Thelma to smash, but I had none.

CHAPTER 22

In early September I took a trip with Zlavik to Uncle David's cabin in Colorado. Almost a year had passed since the campaign.

I was bored and depressed after three days there. I disliked our meals of half-heated beans and canned brown bread. I wasn't amused by his card tricks, nor did I want to learn how to play poker. I did try to read at night, but got headaches from the lantern's kerosene smell.

After ten on the fourth night, Zlavik left for a walk. Seconds later, the door flew open. "Look at this moon."

"I'm tired."

"The time is perfect." Zlavik was shouting. "The rituals...remember?"

I sighed. "I'm not in the mood for your esoteric bullshit."

"Just come out--look at the moon!"

Irritated, I followed him out. The moon's image grabbed me: it was gigantic, glowing with a silver-blue hue. The clear mountain air accented the image even more. "David called this 'the night of the great moon.' He said a gate opens and we can achieve a deeper level of consciousness. Weird huh?" Zlavik smiled as though he were the scoutmaster at a new age boy scout jamboree.

"What do we do?"

"Bay at the moon."

"You're bullshitting me."

"Trust me...you're ripe."

Part of me was interested, yet part said this was some hokum ooga-booga.

"So...what do we do?"

"We each climb up a tree, as high as we can. Find a branch you can stand on. The next step is slow breathing until you feel calm inside. Then you start to howl."

"What the hell--point out a good tree."

"Take that one there--it was one of David's favorites. I'll take one fifty feet away, so we can see each other."

Zlavik climbed his big pine, nimbly, testing each branch before he'd put his weight down. Within moments, he was forty feet up. He held on to the trunk with one arm. His back was to me, and he was fully silhouetted against the moon.

"Ah-ah-ah-oooooo!" he yelled.

I climbed my pine tree. At about ten feet, a branch broke under my foot, but the others held.

"Be careful--Uncle David once fell from that tree," Zlavik said.

"Oh, that's reassuring."

"It's okay, he fell from a lot of trees." He laughed and resumed his howls.

I continued to climb--but gingerly. At twenty feet, I looked down and became aware of my racing heartbeat. I held onto the trunk with both hands, remembering to breathe slowly. I spotted a large supporting branch about ten feet above me. One branch at a time, and I arrived, grasping two overhead branches for extra security. I was thirty feet off the ground. I had room to stand to my full height, but I remained sitting, holding onto the trunk with one hand and the branch with another.

"Don't think about what you're doing--just surrender," Zlavik yelled.

He began another round of his howls. I could hear faint echoes. I felt resentful--I wanted to have the whole area to myself.

I took three breaths, focusing on the moon.

"Ah-ah-ah-oooooo!" I yelled.

"Allen, there's one other thing."

"What?"

"Did I tell you the purpose?"

"No!"

"Make love to the moon!"

"Ah-ah-ah-oooooo!" I let myself enter a new world. "Ah-ah-ah-oooooo!" I stood, releasing one hand. I sensed an opening inside.

Awareness hit me: someone else was in my body. There was a flash of recognition: these sounds were familiar. I'd been in the trees before, cupping my hands to my mouth, growling, and howling at the silver ball. My body was different then, shorter, stockier, and hairy. Allen Ford had disappeared.

The howling went on for hours, at times plaintive and at other times joyful. Zlavik and I took turns alternating our cries in an easy rhythm. I felt weightlessas I howled. The early morning sunlight and singing of birds broke the reverie. I climbed down the tree still in a mild trance. I got to the bottom and embraced the sticky pillar of bark for a long moment. Still charged with the energy, I spent an hour writing in my journal. Fatigue took over and I stumbled into my sleeping bag, a joyous exhaustion filling me. I dreamt of old Alaskan glaciers that had melted and turned into lush, fertile lands--and I was the overseer.

Around noon I awoke to the smell of coffee and the harsh sound of a bird squawking in the nearby brush. Zlavik was cooking on the outdoor stone fireplace. I walked out, in post peak experience reverie. Zlavik appeared tired, but flashed me his big smile and handed me a cup of coffee.

"So, did you make love to the moon?"

"Multiple orgasms all around."

We were quiet as we ate a breakfast of Cheerios, coffee, and oranges. Later, I went off to a secluded clump of trees, notebook in hand. I wanted to write--first hand--of my breakthrough. I recalled the photo I'd seen of a triumphant Harold at Masada. Now I, too, had been catapulted through the keyhole.

"Ah, yes the academic is breaking it down, categorizing, putting it into little labeled bottles." Zlavik was standing behind me looking down.

"Hey, this is my way."

"Hell, you'll probably analyze the whole thing away."

"Okay...my socks and shoes were blown off...I'm still overwhelmed, but my note taking helps me get clear."

In the early 1950's, according to Zlavik, David had a special dream that instructed him to move a particular boulder to the top of the seven-thousand-foot mountain on which he lived. In ten years, David had moved the rock six thousand feet. Zlavik explained that David's dream said he could use rollers and a lever, but no machines. The dream said David would move to another level of consciousness when the stone reached the top.

"I was fourteen when I first saw my uncle spend half of each day sweating and cursing as he struggled to move that stone ten or fifteen feet a day. He'd even piss on the stone when he got mad. I thought he was nuts and ridiculed him by referring to his quest as 'Rocky Mountain Fruitcake Dream.'"

"So?" I said.

Zlavik continued and said his uncle's favorite reply was to cackle and say, 'Boy, everybody is rolling a stone up a mountain like I am. The difference is, mine is visible.' Then he'd cackle again, slap his thighs and go back to work, still laughing.

Zlavik looked at me calmly. "I want the two of us to move the boulder the final one thousand feet."

"You're nuts!" I said. "Go to Colorado and spend our time moving a boulder a thousand feet up a mountain to fulfill some old man's wacko dream?"

"You're raising your voice." Zlavik grinned. "I have a way to speed things up. Just keep an open mind, huh?"

I shook my head while Zlavik took a diagram from his shirt pocket. "Check this out. If we go with my plan, we can get it up the remaining distance working just a few hours a day." The diagram showed a bed of ten logs to roll the rock. "If we used two iron poles, we can move it two hundred feet a day--I did the math. The genius of this is using two poles for added leverage and momentum."

"I'll give it a shot," I said. "But only for a day." We found the boulder two days later, after a vigorous hunt. The rock was about the size of two trunks welded together.

I started our first day feeling resentful. We stripped to our waists and each of us grabbed a large iron pole. We stood five feet apart, wearing gloves and hiking boots for traction. The ten logs were positioned in front of us, creating an easy track.

"Allen, one of my purposes is to push your edges. I believe you've been on vacation for a while."

"So how do we start?"

"You're too agitated now for the right state. We need to do the breathing."

We breathed for several minutes; I decided to let go and give myself to the boulder.

Both of our iron poles clanged against the boulder at the same time, creating sparks--it began moving. We covered ten feet in ten minutes. The experience was effortless.

"The biggest obstacle was you--not the rock."

I nodded. Moving the boulder became our morning ritual during our last week.

On our last day, we had 200 feet left to the summit, and I surprised myself. "I don't care how long it takes, I want to stay here until we get it to the top."

"Boy, what a change. This is a little sick, you know."

We worked steadily the entire day, except for a short lunch break; the sky was clear and a cool breeze helped us endure the afternoon heat. We stopped several more times for short rest breaks and to drink from the tepid water bottle. We were both tiring. It was four p.m. and we had fifty feet to go. I noticed a nearby ledge with a sharp drop off.

"Okay, we get this to the top, and then what happens, Mr. Shaman?" I asked.

Zlavik grinned. "Maybe the act of bringing it up is the gift. David's pet phrase was the 'unity of the paradox,' which I heard many times."

I began jumping up and down and laughing. "I've got it! I've got it!"

"What?" said Zlavik.

"We push the rock over to that ledge and let it roll down to the bottom. That action best expresses paradox."

"No! That defeats the whole purpose! I disagree! I want to leave it at the summit as a memorial to David. We've worked too hard. Your idea doesn't honor our effort."

"Don't you get it? It's so obvious. In letting go of putting the rock on top, we fulfill our mission. It's perfect paradox."

Zlavik's expression softened. I could see him playing and turning the idea around in his head. The wrinkles in his forehead faded.

"Maybe you've got a point. But, damn we worked so hard." He closed his eyes, then opened them with a sudden smile.

"Your idea does express the principle," he laughed. "David would love it!"

We moved the boulder to the ledge and stared at the sharp drop to the bottom.

"Ready...let her go." Both our poles wedged under and lifted the rock simultaneously. We watched and listened as the boulder clattered, clanged and bounced down the mountain side. We slapped and hugged each other as a large dust plume gathered behind the racing boulder.

Chapter 23

Near the end of our vacation, during one of his discourses about his Uncle David, Zlavik mentioned the Darbay, a powerful hallucinogen from the Amazon, that his uncle had used to enhance his spiritual growth. Zlavik told me he'd taken it once, when he was seventeen. He said his preference now was for daily meditation. "My time might be limited, so I want to jumpstart you--even more." His expression grew pinched.

I nodded but remained silent.

"Allen, taking the Darbay is the equivalent of years of devout meditation. It's like the hard-wiring of your brain reconfigures itself."

"Tantalizing thought," I said. "And this public service announcement is brought to you by a former mainstream congressional candidate."

"I want you to use it," Zlavik said, ignoring my comment. "Man, you're opening up big time." He poked me on the shoulder. Then he went to a floorboard near the fireplace and carefully removed one plank. He reached in and pulled out a small, red, dented metal box. He opened it and showed me a long crooked black root, a bit longer than his finger. "This stuff is twenty years old, and it improves with age."

The next day, we stood at a semi-circle of stones that David had set up for rituals. Zlavik had a fresh lemon and squeezed it into boiling water in an open pot on the stone fireplace. "The lemon activates the Darbay." He then cut up three inches of Darbay on a cutting board, dicing it. Bit by bit, he pushed the pieces into the boiling liquid with the edge of his knife. "This will take about fifteen minutes." He chuckled. "Man, you are going on a ride."

Zlavik poured the drink into two tin cups.

"Let it cool down for a few minutes, then gulp it. It'll take about a half hour before it hits you."

I drank the liquid fast before I could change my mind. The bitter taste was like prune juice gone bad. I didn't care. I'd decided to push every edge I knew in my post-Thelma time.

"Hey, it's been half an hour, and all I feel is a slight euphoria," I said. "What's the big deal?"

"Count your breaths," Zlavik said, "just keep counting. Don't rush it." He closed his eyes and leaned against a boulder.

I relaxed, and within a few minutes another change occurred. There was a strange roar that was getting louder and louder. It was if a mega, black Niagara Falls was pulling me into an abyss.

"Zlavik! Help! I'm going under!" I yelled as panic took me.

He opened his eyes, and grabbed both of my hands. "Breathe! Allen, breathe! Focus on the breath, just the breath. Anchor with it!" He repeated the directions while he continued holding both of my hands, synchronizing his breath with mine.

I breathed in slowly in the nose, out the mouth. The undertow began releasing its grip. I was feeling safe again. Zlavik let go my hands. I did my breath count, again, opening myself for the next change. A thin, clear membrane appeared, and I catapulted through it, landing on the ground.

I opened my eyes. Everything looked similar: the rocks, the pine trees, the cabin, the distant snow capped Rockies. But there was a faint, glowing blue light emanating from everything. I knew I was in a parallel reality which lay alongside our own. Waves of euphoria swirled over me.

"Are you there yet?" Zlavik asked.

"Yes."

My whole body opened. *"All is explained in the unity of the paradox."* I knew this was the same voice that had spoken to Zlavik. The authority was unimpeachable.

All my senses were rippling with new powers. I could hear a bird flapping its wings far off in the distance. And I could feel sap oozing from a tree a hundred yards away. I held my hand out in front of me and saw it as translucent, seeing the veins and bone structure revealed.

"You have three hours left," Zlavik said. Let go of boundaries. The Darbay will be your guide."

I took out my notebook. I didn't want to miss anything. I breathed, slowly, for a period of time before the next change occurred. I felt a kaleidoscope turning inside of me. Ahead, on the horizon, was a huge object, which became clearer. It was a moist, huge, pulsating red heart, which kept expanding until it seemed to be the universe, and I was merging into it. Several more hours passed where I went in and out of ecstatic states.

At dusk the effects of the Darbay were wearing off. I walked back to the cabin feeling like a child who had experienced fifty Christmas mornings simultaneously. Zlavik was nowhere in sight, so I took out my journal and wrote as if I was taking dictation from God. I wrote for several hours before falling asleep.

The next morning I awoke feeling tired and sore. I stood up wobbly, grabbing a nearby chair for support. At last, it was clear to me: At the center of all things was a living heart that intersected and unified everything. It was as true as it was invisible. I jumped and laughed for several minutes. 'God-drunk' I remembered a phrase Zlavik used from his Uncle David. I calmed myself and returned to my writing.

Zlavik appeared an hour later and gave me a bear hug. "I watched you. I could tell you had your breakthrough. Your expressions were ecstatic. Damn, you're taking off." He laughed and slapped me on the back.

"You're still afraid to let go--huh?"

"Yeah." I looked away.

"Honor Harold's advice. There is a leap of faith before you can permanently anchor to the other side."

"Did you hear anything about the three tasks?" I asked.

"No. There was just a black iron wall like the Great Wall of China. All I did was go back and forth, tapping for a hollow spot--there was none. I'm stuck now. Bad." He kicked a stone and sent it flying.

I walked over to him. For the first time I realized his pensive side reminded me of Martin's. "There must be a way."

"Thanks. I did see one other thing in my experience."

"What?"

His voice lowered.

"Your heart and head are coming together and I saw you surpassing me--in all ways." Zlavik looked away. "I'm too extreme in all that I do. I'm always going into the red zone. There's a price for that. You've avoided my sins."

Zlavik excused himself and went for a walk. He was gone for several hours. When he returned, he was quiet during dinner, eating only half his meal, and going to bed by nine.

When he was asleep, I reviewed my journal. I'd filled up twenty pages. The Darbay had brought me into the Great Room. Everything in my life had accelerated. An awareness snapped on like baseball stadium lights in pitch black: some kind of plan had always been at work in my life. Somehow everything that ever happened to me was perfect--even Thelma.

Yet I sensed that Zlavik's plan was accelerating in an unnown direction, and that, of course, tempered my elation

CHAPTER 24

On our first Saturday afternoon back at Jackson's Restaurant, Zlavik seemed restless and I let him talk. He said, for the first time, that things were off in his marriage. "We've been drifting apart for at least a year. I'm lucky if we make love once a month. Barbara is still a very private person." He shook his head. "I have to keep pulling things out of her."

He also shared his frustration at work. "Hell, I can coast there for the next twenty years–with both eyes shut." And he added the news that Bruce Michaels was giving him the cold shoulder. "He avoids eye contact, whenever we are at a meeting, and when he thinks I'm not looking, he gives me these quick, sharp looks." Zlavik added he felt like the skunk at the picnic.

One month later there was an irreparable blow-out between the two men. Zlavik said he confronted Bruce about his coldness and Bruce let loose with a barrage of criticism from the affair with Alana, asking him if his seizures were a way he got out of things. Bruce also told him that he probably would end up as a gigolo to some aging heiress in Miami Beach. Zlavik resigned from his position that afternoon.

Three weeks later on a Sunday afternoon, I got a call from a subdued Zlavik. He cleared his throat a number of times, as though someone had a hand around his neck.

"Allen...Barbara and I have made a decision to separate for a trial period. Um...my guess is we will get a divorce, but we're taking it slow."

"I'm sorry, Zlavik. Are you okay?"

"I'm a little scared, but I'm not sure why." He excused himself saying he was going to take a nap.

One hour later, the phone rang and it was Barbara. She was breathing hard and talking between gulps of air. "Zlavik is having an awful seizure...please...I need help."

I drove through two red lights and when I arrived Barbara sobbed and grabbed onto me as if I were the last lifeguard on the beach. Zlavik was laying on the middle of the floor, blacked out after a twenty minute Grand-Mal. The coffee table was overturned, a lamp broken.

Barbara was trembling. "I can't deal with it anymore. There are two people in him, in constant battle. I'm overwhelmed. I feel guilty but I need to separate. Could you and Ollie stay in close contact with him?" she said.

"Sure," I said. At the end of that week she'd moved out of their house.

During the weeks that followed, Zlavik averaged a major seizure every few days. He chipped two of his teeth in one episode. On another day he knocked over his prized Seth Thomas grandfather clock, shattering the face beyond repair.

Either Ollie or I dropped by every other day. Zlavik's skin took on a grayish tone, and he was getting confused about whether he was taking the correct amounts of his medication. "I'm aware I'm losing ground," he said in a low voice.

On one Friday afternoon, when I dropped by, I found him unshaven and still in his red plaid bathrobe. He was thinner and, for the first time, looked older than his thirty-three years.

However, he was eager to talk and I stayed for several hours. "I believe what's going on is my failure to complete the third task," he said. "According to the voice, I had eight years; this is the end of the seventh."

A few days later, I got a call from Ollie. "There was a bad seizure on Saturday. He was flopping like a trout. The episode lasted forty minutes. I understand why Barbara left."

Ollie and I pressured Zlavik to make an appointment with a new neurologist in town. The doctor started him on a whole new regimen of medication. However, Zlavik expressed doubts about their efficacy. "My thinking feels even more cloudy."

Zlavik started to see the wolf again. "Allen, it was three in the morning. I was going to the bathroom and saw it sitting out in the backyard looking up at my window." He said he was taking no chances and had placed his loaded twenty-two rifle under his bed. Zlavik shared one new thought. He said there might be a way out of his crisis, because he now believed that the third task might be killing the wolf. Evidence was pointing towards that fact. A shudder went through his body.

I questioned Zlavik about the guidance from his inner voice. He said he had heard nothing, and added that his major concern was his weakened health. He had given up his daily three mile run and was substituting a short, six-block walk to the neighborhood store. "Hell, I can't even have a decent meditation."

Ollie and I were still alternating our days visiting Zlavik. Each of us would drop by for a few hours in the morning. I asked for help from Maureen Bellows, a neighbor of Zlavik's. Her background as a registered nurse was reassuring.

I wasn't surprised when Ollie called me for lunch and brought up the topic of our friend's health. "Zlavik keeps throwing me for a loop. On the surface he's like this Greek God: looks, charm, build, and intelligence. Then bam, he turns into Humpty Dumpty, falls off the wall, and breaks into a million pieces. And all the king's horses and all the king's men can't put him back together again."

Ollie shook his head. "Even when he's back on the wall smiling, as though nothing has happened, you can sense that the fissures and the crack lines are still there."

I nodded. "I don't know how he does it."

At the end of June, Zlavik's seizures hit critical mass. Maureen called me early on Saturday. "I need you and Ollie over here--fast. Zlavik has had five seizures in the last twenty-four hours. He's disoriented--things are bad."

Ollie and I arrived at the same time. Maureen was in the living room crying. She'd pushed aside all the furniture to make the room safer. Zlavik was on the floor, blacked out.

"Look guys," Maureen said, "this isn't working." Her voice was raspy. "I'm over my head here. His seizures are unlike any I've ever seen before--there's so much anger in them." She wiped her eyes and shook her head. "He told me yesterday that he wants to go out in his canoe. He said, 'If a seizure comes and I fall over the side, so be it. I will have my own version of a Viking funeral.'"

"What do we do?" I asked.

"He's slipping. We need to hospitalize him," Maureen said.

"Jesus," Ollie said a number of times under his breath.

"He hates hospitals," I added. "He was put in one at age twenty. They misdiagnosed the seizures, and he ended up in the state mental hospital for two weeks. He goes phobic at the mention of the word."

Ollie asked, "How about private duty nurses?"

"He needs hospitalization," Maureen said. "If he stays home, he'll be dead in a couple of days."

We agreed to call a local ambulance service to take Zlavik to Westbridge Community Hospital.

Thirty minutes later Zlavik woke up as two attendants lifted him onto the stretcher. He was too weak to resist but he did manage to say, "You bastards," under his breath.

I drove around Westbridge without a destination after I left the house. One year ago Zlavik was positioned to be our next congressman. Six months ago he was my guru in the Rockies, mentoring me to mega peak experiences. Now, he'd become a self-eviscerating Humpty Dumpty. What was real? Once more I felt frozen.

I didn't want to go home. Instead, I drove to Greenfield. I headed straight for the South Cemetery. I drove as close as I could to Martin's gravestone and walked the remaining distance. I sat down near the stone, the ground was damp, the sky overcast. I sat cross-legged for half an hour but only felt colder and more alone.

I walked back to my car and drove to my parents' home. The house was dark and my parent's car was gone. I parked in the driveway, went to the back door and found the spare key and let myself into the house. I moved fast as I went upstairs and opened the door to the attic. Passing the dust-covered boxed train set in the corner, I lifted up the floor board, and retrieved the Bowie knife from its twenty year crypt. Intuition told me I needed the knife back.

I returned home at around eight that night. I did laundry, dishes, and even vacuumed the first floor. Around midnight, I put Johnny Carson on and watched the show till one. Before going to bed, I brought the trash out to my barrels in the backyard.

Out of the dark I heard an unfamiliar, menacing growl from the woods which bordered my lawn. It was unlike any I heard before. I retreated back to the house and locked all the doors and windows. I repeated to myself that it was some stray dog, but I took the Bowie knife and placed it on the bed stand before I went to bed.

CHAPTER 25

Maureen had been on staff at the Westbridge Community Hospital and knew Dr. Beechum, the Chief Physician. The scenario was for Zlavik to stay in critical care for two weeks until they stabilized him.

I called Zlavik's mother Nadine to inform her. Her speech was slurred: "So what the hell am I supposed to do...he's pulled this shit before." She hung up.

Nancy, Zlavik's younger sister, was quiet when I called her; she said she would fly out to see him.

Only Maureen was allowed in the intensive care unit to see Zlavik. She checked in with me the next day. "He's heavily medicated," she said. "Their first goal is getting the seizures under control. He's still having three or four a day, but the severity has lessened."

"Anything else?" I asked.

"He growls sometimes during his seizures. The nurses have nicknamed him "werewolf."

Two days later, halfway through my summer class, Ollie burst into my classroom. "There's an emergency"--Ollie's face was flushed and his shirt was covered in sweat.

"What is it?" I asked in the hallway.

"All hell has broken loose--Zlavik walked out of the hospital--in his jonny. He said he was going home. They sent the cops after him."

I kicked the wall.

Ollie continued. "Zlavik fought them off," Ollie said, "until they maced him, put him in a strait jacket, and took him to the State Mental Hospital in Hartford. Maureen is beside herself."

I kicked the door again.

"Shit! Why did this have to happen?" I dismissed my class, aware of their startled expressions. My memory of my own trip to the Albany hospital and the panic I felt, came to my mind.

Ollie and I took off and met Maureen at Jackson's Restaurant. She was sitting there smoking, eyes rimmed with red.

"What do you know?" I asked.

"It was awful." Maureen related how Zlavik woke up that morning and was conscious for the first time.

Zlavik told the staff he hated hospitals. Dr. Beechum explained how close to death he had been. Zlavik was quiet as the doctor spoke. After the doctor left and everything seemed to be okay, Zlavik, with nothing on but his jonny, walked out of the hospital.

The police were called. Dr. Beechum instructed them to take Zlavik to the state hospital under the Emergency Detention Law.

Ollie asked, "What's that?"

Maureen lit another cigarette. "The state can involuntarily commit a person for three days if they are a risk to themselves."

Maureen snuffed out her cigarette and told us the current legal status. "Under state law, there must be a hearing in three days, and the burden of proof is on the party committing him."

"So what do we do?" Ollie asked.

Maureen caught my eyes with her tired ones. She told us if he was committed for a longer period, we could then try to get him transferred into a private hospital. The strategy would buy him time. "By the way, all of us will have to testify at the hearing." She said Zlavik had been jeopardizing his life with erratic doses of his medications due to his impaired thinking. "If we can't extend the three days, anything is possible."

I went home. My thinking kept spinning around one question: had I let down another brother? Later, I went back to my den, lit a cigar, and popped open a beer. There was even a pull to call Thelma. She'd been insightful and compassionate at times. The scene with her flying the red kite on the Bermuda bluff came back. I'd never seen her so happy. I finished the beer, but my thoughts were still heavy: a brother could die--again--and I seemed incapable of reversing the chain of events.

Then I considered Charlotte. I hadn't told her all the details of Zlavik's descent over the last months, and I hadn't returned her calls of the last week. I was avoiding her and, at the same time, wishing for her presence.

I tried to blow rings with my cigar as Harold had. I recalled my questions again from college: What is true? What is real? And what is the damn purpose?

My testimony in court would be damning if I revealed Zlavik's previous sentence at twenty. Once more he would feel betrayed by those closest to him. I snuffed out my cigar, burning my fingers.

Memories of Martin's last year surfaced: out of nowhere the scene with the dogs jolted me from my chair.

Chapter 26

The hearing was held in the District Court Building in Hartford. Maureen, Ollie and I went there together, and had little difficulty finding the dirty brick building. We took our seats in the back of the dark, oak paneled second floor room.

The clerk called "State of Connecticut vs. Zlavik Johnson." A side door opened and Zlavik entered, dressed neatly in casual khaki slacks and a forest green polo shirt. He appeared at ease and confident--as if he had just returned from the archery range. I was startled when I saw Ian MacDonald walk in and sit next to him. The two men hugged each other. Zlavik shot a suspicious look at me.

Zlaviks' attorney, appointed by the court, stood up to address the judge. "Your honor," he said, looking disheveled in a baggy, brown, three-piece suit. "We ask that the court dismiss the charges." He turned, glancing at Zlavik. "My client has a long-term seizure disorder. He was hospitalized against his will, and many of his actions were misinterpreted."

Maureen was called first. After fifteen minutes of testimony, she concluded with, "Your honor, I am convinced that without Zlavik's hospitalization, he would be dead."

Zlavik's attorney interrupted. "Are you a psychiatric nurse?" he asked.

"No."

"So your overall assessment is the opinion of a lay person?"

Maureen's jaw dropped. "Look, I've had fifteen years of varied nursing experience. I know what I saw."

"Nonetheless, you're not certified to give a formal mental health assessment?"

"No, but..."

"Thank you. That's all, Your Honor."

Ollie was next. His shirt betrayed large sweat marks under the arms as he walked to the witness stand.

"What are your professional credentials, Mr. Stevenson?" Zlavik's attorney asked.

"I'm a historian with a Ph.D. in American History."

"Is history considered a science, Mr. Stevenson?"

"Well, uh, no. The interpretation of facts is pretty subjective."

"So, Mr. Stevenson, logically, your interpretation of the facts of this case are also probably subjective? Is that true?"

Ollie mumbled a hesitant, "Yes," and then turned red-faced as the attorney hit him with a series of follow-up questions. The attorney excused him as a witness. The lawyer smiled at Zlavik like a pompous Perry Mason getting ready for the final denouement. Ollie's upper shirt was drenched.

I was the last witness. After I was sworn in, I sat down and stared straight at Zlavik. I wanted him to know I was coming from a place of honor, but he looked away.

My mouth was dry and my throat tight as I ticked off the events of last year and their cumulative effect on Zlavik's life. I mentioned the job loss, the divorce, the lost election, the increase in seizures and the depression. The moment I said the word "depression," Zlavik's attorney objected.

"Mr. Ford, do you have any clinical credentials in the field of medicine, psychiatry, or psychology?"

"No. My doctorate is in religion and psychology."

"Well, then, Mr. Ford," he said, turning again to face the judge. "Once more, having no clinical credentials, we must object to a lay person using the clinical term, depression."

"Look, I don't have to be a clinical psychologist to recognize this," I said. "The criteria for depression are readily available in books."

"Mr. Ford, this is a hearing to determine the mental condition of Mr. Johnson. As his friend, I'm sure you don't want to provide testimony that isn't scientific." The attorney asked the judge to excuse me. The judge nodded.

I returned to my seat next to Ollie. I looked over at Zlavik, his head bent close to Ian's. They were talking in an animated fashion.

I elbowed Maureen. "Look at him," I whispered. "He's acting like this is a minor traffic ticket. Four days ago, he was running down Main Street with a jonny on."

"We'll have a short recess," the judge said.

Zlavik leaned back in his chair, his arms stretched. He seemed to be relishing the entire hearing as if it were a chess game. His old, confident self was back.

The judge reentered in less than ten minutes. He gaveled the room to order.

"We are dismissing the case against Zlavik Johnson due to a lack of substantive evidence. Mr. Johnson, you are free to go."

Zlavik stood and hugged his attorney and slapped Ian on the back. His smile was electric.

"I'm afraid for him," Maureen said.

"I hope I never see him again," I said.

"It's okay...it's okay...," said Ollie, as he patted my back out in the hall. I felt tired and heavy on the ride back to Westbridge.

At home, I decided to level a large slope in my backyard. I dug in fast and hard, heaving shovel after shovelful into a growing pile twenty feet away. I ranted to myself as I slung the dirt: "The three tasks never existed! The voice wasn't real. And the giant wolf was bullshit!" Zlavik was a self-immolating con-man whose three-ring circus had finally gone bankrupt.

I kept shoveling until dusk when I took a short break. A smell hit my nostrils: a sharp, unpleasant, sulphurous odor. I felt an immediate clamping sensation in my stomach. I could hear movement in the woods that backed up against my yard. Spontaneously, the hair on my back and arms stood-up. Some kind of primitive alarm system was clanging inside. A large animal was moving thirty feet from where I stood. Instinct showered me with adrenalin, as I ran into the house, bolted all the doors and locked the windows. My heart was pounding, and I discovered I was still holding the shovel. The state of alarm persisted.

I went to the refrigerator, grabbed a beer, and repeatedly looked out of my den slider into the backyard in the early evening darkness. By the third beer, the fear had lessened, but I kept pacing back and forth between my kitchen and den, still looking out my windows.

The thought came to me that I wanted to give another speech from Townsend Towers. It would be a twelve year update. I'd start with a paraphrase of Sartre's famous quote. "Hell is having a brother."

I lit a cigar, opened another beer and continued my reverie as I paced. Once more I was out on the balcony of Townsend Tower. I launched into my update of reality at age thirty-three to my fellow M.F.C. alumni.

First, I gave an apology to Ty-Ty. Due to the fact that life was a meaningless crap shoot, more of us should race mopeds in buildings at ungodly hours. Second, we should have a new national holiday called "Larry Erskine Day." On this day everyone would be allowed to throw three coat hangers at anyone they disliked. And I proposed that Professor Niel's birthday be celebrated as a national holiday known as NOK-Day, to remind us all that *no one knows what's going on.*

Then I spotted a picture of Zlavik and me at the archery range. I removed the photo from the frame and touched the tip of my cigar to the edge. A brown color spread across the curling photo.

I noted the weathered picture of Martin on my bookcase, grabbed it, and shoved it into my bottom desk drawer—face down. I wanted no reminders of either of my two brothers.

CHAPTER 27

Rumors flew after Zlavik's release. Many had to do with Zlavik suing Ollie, Maureen, Dr. Beechum, and me. Huge sums of money were mentioned. There was also a rumor that his house was up for sale. A few people said that he was moving back to Seattle and only renting his house.

Two facts were clear. Nancy, Zlavik's sister, had flown in to stay with him, and Nick Garibaldi was stopping by with two of his sons on a daily basis. Zlavik had met Nick at the newsstand he owned and they had become friends. Ollie was my main source of information. He still dropped by to pick up his newspaper at Nick's stand, and was gleaning gossip.

Perhaps the most compelling item was how Ian MacDonald had befriended Zlavik. Ian had wanted a story to follow-up his original pieces, and had interviewed Zlavik at the state hospital. However, the interview hadn't gone as he'd expected. Zlavik broke down and spilled his guts. MacDonald was moved, and he promised Zlavik he would help him get out.

Ollie related what was happening in Zlavik's life in regular meetings at Jackson's Restaurant. He said that after his court release Zlavik received his first shock. "It was Saturday night and his new coterie of friends were at his house having a spaghetti supper. At about nine that night, Zlavik excused himself saying he heard a noise in the backyard. They heard his yell when he found what was left of Palmer, his cat. The cat had been mutilated beyond recognition, tufts of cat fur were everywhere."

Zlavik lost it, Ollie explained. "He ran to his bedroom and grabbed his twenty-two. Before he left he managed to give his new friends the background on the wolf. Next he told everyone he wouldn't return until the 'thing' was dead, and headed for the woods behind his house. Two gunshots were fired fifteen minutes later."

Ollie sipped from his water and continued the story. He said Zlavik returned at midnight, telling everyone that he saw the wolf, but it had escaped. He then went to his room, pulled all the shades down, and said he needed to be alone. He stayed up all night sitting in a wooden rocker and fingering a piece of leather left over from the cat's collar.

Nancy, Zlavik's sister, had also updated Ollie. She explained that her brother had done something similar in high school. He refused to eat, didn't talk, and it went on for days. Nancy was concerned because the seizures were starting to reoccur. Her other worry was that she needed to leave at the end of the week. She didn't know who was going to provide daily support.

Zlavik's withdrawal, she said, lasted for four days. On Thursday, she got up and found him in the kitchen making breakfast. When she walked in, he turned and apologized, explaining that Palmer had been given to him by David and was part of his life for fourteen years. Zlavik broke down, saying the showdown with the wolf was inevitable.

Later in the day his mood picked-up. Ollie said, "He mowed the lawn, washed his car, and vacuumed the downstairs. His color was better and he bantered with Nancy. He was more like his old self."

On Friday, Zlavik got up early and made omelets, Ollie related. Unlike the day before though, he was quiet. "He told Nancy he had a dream that the wolf was on Rose Island, which was about one mile off the coast. The island was a heavily wooded nature preserve. Nancy said he hugged and kissed her several times."

Ollie explained that Nancy then went to the supermarket, and when she returned to the house at noon, she found a note on the kitchen table that said Zlavik had taken the canoe and his twenty-two to Rose Island to kill the wolf. He added if he wasn't back by six to call the police.

"Nancy wanted to call someone but held off. By five, the wind had picked up and the water had an uprising of swells and whitecaps. The sky had darkened with threatening rain clouds. She first called me, saying he'd been gone for five hours."

Ollie then reminded me about the events that happened before we met at Masons Beach, and how I had called the Coast Guard and police.

"The Coast Guard is sending their thirty-eight footer out to Rose Island," I said, "and the police are going to search the shoreline. They brought scuba divers with them. Who knows what's going to happen."

By seven that evening, a small crowd had gathered. The surf and swells were still rough, and the sky was even more ominous. I spotted a red object about a hundred feet off shore. I swallowed several times, then elbowed Ollie.

"See that red thing, I think that's Zlavik's canoe."

We both waded out up to our waists, shivering all the way, to retrieve the upside down canoe. I noticed the Old Town label on the right front and side. "Zlavik's," I said. Ollie remained speechless. We dragged it up to the beach and waved over a police officer.

Nancy approached, saw the canoe and sobbed. Ollie stepped over and comforted her. My own insides were becoming a compacted ice field.

A reporter from WERZ came over and held a microphone near my face. "Aren't you Allen Ford, the former chair of Zlavik's campaign?"

I pushed the man aside and walked toward the other end of the beach, dragging Ollie with me.

We both spotted a familiar, gray haired, figure in a light blue windbreaker walking towards us: Bruce Michaels. He hollered, "I've been hearing the reports on the radio--what do you know?"

"We found his canoe," I said.

He shook his head. Then he headed back to the parking lot, hands in his pockets.

I went home--empty, numb and cold. I grabbed the one and only beer left. I downed it, then lit a cigar. I dialed the New York City telephone number for Thelma, who screamed when I told her.

"I just knew something like this would happen--I just knew it."

We talked for half an hour. Thelma was either crying or laughing. She told me she was seeing another psychiatrist, and they were trying out a new medication. "They think I might be manic-depressive," she said.

As our conversation wound down, she said, "I have one more confession." She began sobbing. "Oh, Allen this is so hard!" There were some more garbled sounds. "I got pregnant during our honeymoon. There was no way I could've been ready for that baby and I was afraid you'd be angry with me so I got an abortion. Allen that's why I pushed so hard for another child--you never got it."

I hung up on her. For the first time in my life I felt old.

CHAPTER 28

We decided to hold a memorial service the following Sunday. The consensus was that strong currents had taken Zlavik's body out to sea.

Nancy was staying on for another week to help organize the service. I'd given her the names of those closest to her brother. I cringed when she told me that Nadine, Zlavik's mother, was flying out.

Quite a few people showed up at the planning meeting: Ollie, Maureen, Bruce, Barbara, Ian, Nick, Alice, Nadine, and myself. We discussed what photos we would use at the service, and almost everyone mentioned having a favorite one. I felt pangs about burning the archery range picture, but said nothing.

Bruce told us that he had arranged for the service to be conducted at the large Congregational church on the downtown green and for a reception to be held at the Westbridge Country Club. He told our group to "spare no expense."

The Saturday of the memorial service was a pristine, August day with a cobalt blue sky. I got up at six and vacuumed the entire house, and still managed to arrive two hours early. On one part of the green, near the church entrance, were all the kids, thirty-six strong, from the Westbridge Children's Home, where Zlavik had been a volunteer. They were standing in a semi-circle, rehearsing a song.

I was enveloped in a hug from Bill Kramer, one of the most enthusiastic volunteers in Zlavik's campaign. "We've got one hundred and twelve precinct chairs here. They all wanted to come. Do you realize seventeen of these people are now running for some kind of local office?"

I nodded and smiled, but remained silent because I'd just flashed back to the service for Martin.

"Zlavik would love this," I finally said. My throat was tight. Part of me wanted to kick or smash something and another part of me wanted to bolt. Inside, I sensed a cauldron of wildly fermenting feelings. Repeatedly, I stuffed the urge to cry.

I turned and saw dozens of faces from the Cabot Insurance Company. Alana Colby passed by and we gave each other hesitant looks. Through the open doors in the center of the church, I saw Bruce Michaels' giving directions, greeting people, and generally being the ringmaster. It was as though he was using his large frame to anchor the whole show.

The local cable TV company was there, getting ready to record the service. Nick Garibaldi waved as he walked by me, surrounded by his entire clan. I was surprised to meet a half dozen students of mine, who had been involved in the campaign. They greeted me tentatively, sensing my tension. There were many other faces I'd never seen before.

Dressed elegantly in a dark blue tailored suit, Charlotte walked up to me and kissed me on the cheek. "This must be so hard for you." She gave her familiar stoic smile and went inside. I was glad she was here.

Sunlight streamed through the church's large side windows. The pulpit was on a raised dais with a huge rosette stained glass window as a backdrop.

A familiar hand touched my shoulder. Turning around, I saw Thelma's blotched face. "I had to come," she said. "He was like a brother to me too. Oh Allen, I'm so sorry about everything."

She blew her nose and I gave her a restrained hug. She took a seat beside Barbara. When another hand touched my back, I knew it was Uncle Harold and we embraced. I excused myself and walked towards the dais. I saw the dozens of floral arrangements on the dais and stopped to read one card, "I will never forget your bravery at the press conference."

The floor began to shake from the surging of the church organ as it began the opening chorus.

The memorial service started on time. Bruce Michaels spoke first.

"Zlavik Johnson was an extraordinary human being. I once told him he had more talent than anyone I'd ever met. His work was both unique and of high quality. He created an in-house daycare program that has become a national model. I want to apologize to him, because..." Bruce hesitated. "I'll miss him," he said and he sat down.

Nick Garibaldi was next: "I came here today because Zlavik Johnson was so different. We opened two more newsstands because he loaned me the money." Nick bowed his head. "Very few people know he had a healing gift. My three-year-old granddaughter, Maria, had leukemia.

One day he put his hands on her head and prayed. Three months later the leukemia was gone. No coincidence--Zlavik did it."

Nick began to cry.

"I don't care if he made mistakes! We all do! He saved my granddaughter's life!"

A strong wave of applause erupted from the crowd as Nick sat down.

As I approached the pulpit scenes of Martin being mauled by the dogs appeared before me leaving me dizzy. I grabbed the pulpit with both hands; the swarm of faces in front of me seemed surreal.

I tried some slow breathing. I looked up and saw Charlotte and Thelma--on opposite sides--nodding at me. "Shakespeare said there were three kinds of greatness. Some men are born great, some men earn it, and some men have it thrust upon them. Zlavik Johnson had all three."

My throat began to lock up. I put my speech back in my coat pocket. I closed my eyes and took more breaths. I think a minute passed.

I opened my eyes, smiled and made eye contact with the audience, who in turn, smiled back. I was in the church--again-- and my purpose was clear.

"Twenty-one years ago I lost my brother, Martin, in a horrific accident. I now realize I've spent most of my life looking for another brother, as well as an explanation for that event. In Zlavik Johnson, I found both. There are windows now cut into my soul, and the new light renews me."

I looked up and saw my mother and father sitting in the right hand back of the church. My mother was crying. My father had an arm around her, he was smiling and giving me the thumbs up.

"Lies!" A tall, skinny white bearded man yelled from the back row. "All the praise about Zlavik. You don't know him the way I do." Two ushers moved towards the man and escorted him out of the church. At the same time Bruce Michaels signaled the choir to begin Zlavik's favorite hymn, "Amazing Grace." The cavernous church filled with the hymn. One by one people linked arms around each other's shoulders; we were all connected, bodies swaying back and forth, unified by the music. We were like the one joined heart I experienced on the Darbay.

I spent at least an hour at the back of the church greeting people. "You've come into your power," my father whispered to me, as he hugged me for the first time in my life.

Part of me, though, couldn't forget the white-haired speaker who had disrupted the service. I knew it was Zlavik's Uncle David and I knew he had valuable information unique only to him.

CHAPTER 29

More than five hundred people came to the reception at the Westbridge Country Club.

Michaels grabbed Ollie and me when we arrived. "I brought the crazy guy who disturbed the service here. He's David Kettner, Zlavik's uncle. Can you go to the conference room to talk to him? He was drinking, but we've given him a lot of coffee."

In the conference room David was slumped back in a chair at the end of the long table. Nancy and Nadine were flanking him, all three in deep conversation. Bruce had assigned Ollie to the room to ride shotgun.

I sat down at the table, and Bruce remained standing. "Mr. Kettner," he said. "I got the police to release you. Naturally, I expect an explanation and any information you may have about the rumors that your nephew may have faked his death."

"That's fair enough," David said. He poured himself water from a glass pitcher, took a long drink, and smacked his lips as he set down the glass.

"I knew Zlavik better than anyone--especially you, Nadine. The fact is I saved that boy from you."

Nadine scowled and folded her arms.

"He didn't die," he said. "No, sir. He's taken off. The boy is too cunning--he'd never do something impulsive."

Nadine sat up. "I disagree. Zlavik would never put his family and friends through such an ordeal!"

David looked at his sister with mock compassion. "Of course he could, my dear. The boy wasn't the same since he took the Darbay. I made a serious mistake giving it to him when he was only seventeen."

"Why are you here?" I asked.

"I have unfinished business with Zlavik. It took me a year to find him, then I subscribed to the local newspaper to follow the campaign." He said we saw only the charismatic do-gooder, a familiar pattern over the years, where Zlavik manipulated people for his own ends--and then took off.

I hit the table.

"Zlavik never once criticized you--why are you so bitter?"

"Someone's got to tell the truth." David took another long drink from the water glass. "I will not let him con anyone--he's my son."

"Don't say such things!" Nadine screamed, and she knocked over her chair and left the room, followed by Nancy.

Bruce Michaels rolled his eyes. "What the hell is this Darbay stuff?"

"A powerful hallucinogen used by native Brazilians to induce mystical states," I said.

"That might explain a few things," Bruce said, as he shook his head.

David turned towards Bruce. "When Zlavik took the Darbay, it brought out his shadow side, because he attacked me verbally--for the first time. There was a viciousness in the boy's tone that was new."

I interrupted. "Cut to the chase."

"Some of you know about the wolf, right?" David looked around and I nodded. He told us that within a week after Zlavik took the Darbay, the wolf showed up at the cabin--for the first time. "I shot the wolf with my bow, but the animal took off with the arrow sticking out from it's chest. Zlavik was nowhere to be found."

One hour later, he said, Zlavik returned to the cabin acting withdrawn and distant. "If I hadn't done a lot of reading on the subject, I never would've given it a second thought."

"What the hell are you getting at?" Bruce shouted.

David cleared his throat, "There's a relationship between Zlavik and the wolf. The creature appears when Zlavik is angry." David said both could be in your presence simultaneously. He also said Zlavik's energy field somehow released the wolf without him being aware of it. And he added that it was important to remember that the wolf and Zlavik were connected and yet two distinct entities. "The wolf could even attack and kill Zlavik. The wolf is Zlavik and it isn't Zlavik. I know the whole thing sounds paradoxical."

"This is the biggest bullshit story I've ever heard!" Bruce yelled. "Your whole family represents a blackhole in the gene pool!" He got up and walked to the window.

"If I get the math right, you've been gone fifteen years, right?" asked Ollie.

"Correct."

"How did all this begin?"

"Well, Zlavik and I were in the habit of climbing trees to bay at the moon. On one particular night, we got into an awful fight after I told him it would be our last summer together." Zlavik, he said, had gone off for a long walk, while he'd climbed his favorite tree.

David related that around midnight, he spotted the wolf for the second time. "The beast was huge and circled the tree I was in. I waited it out and the wolf left--sometime around daylight. I started to come down from the tree. Halfway down I missed a branch and fell. I woke up without a clear memory. All I knew was that I was in danger and had to leave."

David paused to drink some more water. "I ended up in northern California and was able to make a living there as a short order cook. About two years ago, my memory began to return and I started tracing Zlavik's activities."

"You expect us to believe you?" I asked.

"Yes."

"Everyone thought you were dead."

"So."

"Did Zlavik suspect that you were still alive?"

"I think the thought tantalized him," David cackled.

I groaned. "I don't get it, you're too harsh on Zlavik." I was shouting. "Something isn't adding up."

"Let me answer you in a different way." David closed his eyes for a few moments, then opened them. He explained that Zlavik was only seventeen when he first took the Darbay. His reading on the subject revealed he'd made a mistake. "No one under thirty should take it. Zlavik's personality wasn't complete. The drug allowed his shadow side an equal amount of power. The result was that his dark side broke off and expressed itself in the form of the wolf." David said increasing seizures were confirmation of the on-going conflict between the two identities.

"The boy has been on a collision course with himself ever since." David started to digress about unity and paradox until Bruce again exploded from the position he had taken by the window.

"Shadow self, Brazilian hallucinogens, giant wolves, unity, and paradox, you're talking tommyrot. And this from a man who doesn't know where he was for fifteen years!"

I decided to change the direction. "If Zlavik were alive, where would he go?"

David thought for a moment, then scratched his head. "The boy had a penchant for warm weather. I'd guess he'd head for the Southwest."

"How conscious is he about what he's doing?" I asked.

"I'm not sure," David answered while pulling on his beard. "There might be some memory loss. Then again, the boy is so damn awake. Anyway, after the commotion he created here, I suspect he'll keep a low profile."

"What will happen to Zlavik with these two warring sides duking it out?" Ollie asked.

David smiled. "Now that's a dandy question. I believe the boy is stuck now--real bad. The thing is a toss-up, fifty-fifty."

"Is there anyway to help?" I asked.

David said if he could get to Zlavik, he knew some practices that might help. "The other alternative was to kill the wolf." David said the wolf had two objectives: either to kill Zlavik or kill those he loved. He added, " The whole thing represents multiple paradoxes that I'm still struggling to comprehend." I smiled a sardonic smile to myself as I remembered the message of the Darby: *Everything is explained in the unity of the paradox."*

I told David about the three tasks and the voice that guided Zlavik. "Do you think they're true?" I asked.

David cackled again. "Zlavik's so clever, he could convince himself of anything. The boy loved to trifle with the truth." His face tightened. "No, I don't believe he had any special tasks."

Our group left, Ollie staying with David. Nadine got drunk at the bar after Bruce Michaels dismissed her advances with a scathing rebuke.

"Madam, it's amazing that your son survived given the fact you were his mother. I'd have drowned myself by the first grade."

Nadine simply turned her attention to Charlie Madden, who had spent the better part of the evening apologizing to people for his now infamous photograph. Charlie even grabbed hold of me, asking for help in evading Nadine.

Ollie was left alone to watch David, who excused himself to go to the men's room. After ten minutes, Ollie went looking for David and found an open window with an upside down trash can under it. No one reported seeing him leave.

"Shit!" Bruce Michaels shouted when he got the news. He said he'd pay a large sum of money to have David and Nadine stuffed into a sealed metal cylinder which would be dropped into the middle of the Atlantic. "Perhaps when Atlantis surfaces again, they could be reunited with their ancestors."

Later I found time to take a walk out on the golf course with Charlotte. We walked easily with our arms around each other's waists. Everything flowed with her, even our walking pace was effortless. We kissed and hugged gently near the eighth hole and I asked her if we could begin to spend more time together. I apologized for ignoring her calls but she said she understood and accepted my apology. She put her arms on my shoulder, and made eye contact. "I've waited five years...you're good for a short extension." She gave me a wink. We lingered by her car and I gave her several long kisses before she left. I knew our time would be coming--soon.

One hour later, I went outside the country club's entrance and joined a small crowd of a dozen people or so who were milling about. We were there only a minute when we heard wails and screams.

"God, it's Thelma," I said.

There, coming from the parking lot, was a flailing figure in an electric blue dress. She was crying, yelling, and howling as she ran toward us shoeless.

She plowed into my arms. Burying her face in my chest, she enveloped me in her arms, all the time, crying and sobbing.

"It was terrible. So terrible! And big--like a lion!" She shook and sobbed more. "I was scared...so scared."

The heavy oak entrance doors to the country club flew open, and Bruce Michaels' authoritative voice boomed out. "What the hell is going on?"

Thelma stiffened, "Don't patronize me Michaels! I saw a fucking giant wolf, and if you think I'm making it up, I'll show you my wet pants."

Bruce turned to a security guard and asked the man to check the woods near the parking lot where she'd been. Thelma continued to hold on to me.

When the security guard returned he said he searched the area and could find no tracks or anything unusual--except a sulphur-like smell.

I took Thelma back inside and linked her up with Uncle Harold and Marion. All four of us went to the conference room, where Thelma repeated her story of the wolf to her concerned aunt and uncle. Harold looked older and Marion seemed thinner. Harold walked outside the room with me. "I know you kept your promise to me." He paused and broke into a smile. "I can tell you've looked through the keyhole." He kissed me on the forehead and went back to the room.

Ollie and I left the country club near midnight. We talked for a while as we leaned against our cars, exhausted. Then Alice Farnsworth strolled towards us, hands in pockets. "What a day," she muttered. She gave each of us a quick hug. "You two are probably ready for a long vacation. Before I leave, I have one question: Did Zlavik complete the three tasks?" She scanned our faces.

Ollie pointed to me. "He's the resident expert."

"Christ," I said. "I don't want to do this anymore."

"Please," she said. "I value your insight."

I told Alice that I thought Zlavik had completed two of his tasks. The first was his considerable contributions at work. The second was the campaign and how he brought hundreds of people into the political process. I said the third task was never clear to Zlavik, although he once said it might be our friendship--but I doubted that.

"I heard Zlavik say that killing the wolf was the third, but obviously he didn't succeed," Ollie added.

I explained to Alice that Zlavik thought he had eight years to live. Seven had gone by. "Worsening seizures signaled he had failed."

Alice smiled. "I have my own interpretation about things. My God, the man's childhood and adolescence occurred in a charnal house. His dreams and his demons were so intersected that even he didn't know what was fact and what was fable. I believe his experience of the voice and the creation of the three tasks, were a trick of his psyche. Given his history he needed a great melodrama to spur himself on."

I shrugged.

"Here's another wrinkle," Alice said. "Given the extreme stresses of the last year, he could've entered a type of amnesia called a fugue. Even in that state, he was capable of faking a death, creating a new identity, and leaving for a different part of the country."

"He drowned!" I shouted. "I'm sick of all the speculations. He's dead--the show is over!"

CHAPTER 30

"Will they ever find his body? Was there a conspiracy? Was he working for the CIA? Did he have amnesia? Do you think he's alive?"

People would ask me those questions wherever I went in the year following Zlavik's death. Even some of my students were hooked. I'd force a smile and say that I believed he'd drowned. Fueling the questions was a flurry of alleged Zlavik sightings. One volunteer from the campaign swears she saw Zlavik hitchhiking on the Merritt Parkway on the afternoon he disappeared. Bruce Michaels' sister, Pat, said she saw a circus performance in Copenhagen that fall with a clever clown who's build and body language were a twin of Zlavik's. Ollie's parents were vacationing in Vancouver and caught a glimpse of a bearded excursion boat captain who bore a strong resemblance. I found the reports unsettling.

On the six month anniversary of Zlavik's disappearance, Bruce Michaels asked me to lunch. I knew he had private investigators doing research for him. We discussed the rumored sightings, and we also talked about the State Attorney General's investigation which had been released a month earlier. The report said that Zlavik, probably, had a seizure and fell overboard.

"I was upset," said Bruce. "These reports were coming in on the average of one new one a week--it's like those Elvis sightings." He told me he'd hired a crack New York City private investigation agency four months ago, to run down leads. "I've spent over seventy thousand dollars on the search, even flying one investigator to Denmark to interview the clown my sister saw. All the leads turned up empty."

Bruce also said he'd been checking out leads about Uncle David's whereabouts. "The son-of-a-bitch loon must have beamed back up to the mother ship--there is no trace of him," he said.

He handed me the agency's eighty page report. "They had two guys working on this full-time. Every possible lead was run down...no way can Zlavik be alive."

On the way home from lunch, my thoughts turned to Charlotte. After the memorial service, we took a one week vacation to Cape Cod. On our second night there we were walking on the beach by the light of a huge, full moon. We spent an hour sitting on a sand dune holding each other and looking out at the view.

The light of the moon had forged a shimmering silver path--almost to our feet. A steady surf provided an audio counterpart. "I get a little crazy," I said, "when there is a full moon." I howled several times. We both laughed and embraced.

"Let's get married!" We both said it at the same time.

On the way back to the car, Charlotte whispered in my ear. "Thelma was a fool to lose you." I smiled.

Six months later we were married. We bought a house a few blocks from Mason's Beach and three months later Charlotte was pregnant. We both sensed it would be a boy and I was given the task of choosing a name. I had no hesitation: Zlavik Martin Ford.

We got busy remodeling the house and creating a real baby's room. There was a flow with Charlotte that I never had with Thelma. We would slip into an almost daily conjoined belly laugh over mundane things: like our shower curtain that never stayed up, or our tea kettle with the strange whistle. This time I knew I had a partner for life.

On the way to work I'd drive by Zlavik's house. Sometimes I'd tense up, remembering the last few months of his life; at other times I'd smile, wave--like part of him still lived there. As time passed, the sight of his house caused me less pain and I'd just smile and wave.

In May of 1985, as I turned thirty-five, I took up a new physical fitness regimen. I started jogging a five mile route every other day. On the in-between days I would do an hour's workout with small hand weights. The cross-training effects felt good. I sensed I was losing weight with the new routine.

Intuitively, I felt other changes being set in motion. Once a week I went to the archery range to keep my skills fresh. And I even joined an adult soccer league.

At the end of twelve weeks, I stood in front of a full-length mirror with only my running shorts on. I'd lost twelve pounds and noticed more definition. The reflection felt good to me as a man turning thirty-five.

Charlotte walked by and caught me preening. "Something tells me your regimen has to do with those new gray hairs I've spotted." She smiled and brushed her hands over my temples. "Then again, you may want to be in excellent shape for holding this baby of ours. I think it's going to be big." Charlotte took her hands from her stomach, laughed and grabbed my biceps. "Tarzan, how about bringing this laundry basket downstairs?"

On my way downstairs I yelled to her, "I'm in training for I know not what." The statement surprised me as I headed down the stairs. In a way, I felt like I too, had an embryo inside, but I couldn't identify its purpose or nature. I just knew I needed to carry it to term.

I began meditation in the morning and I saw results after three months. I was going to a deeper level. There were several moments, when as Zlavik described, I entered through the gap and rested in spaces of startling serenity.

"I've never seen you so peaceful." Both Charlotte and Ollie commented on my new state. Over and over I discovered the breath was the master key. I could feel my practice blossoming.

In one of my deeper meditative states, I heard a message, *"You're going to complete your brother's mission."* The voice was like the one I experienced on the Darbay. The authority was startling. I tried to dismiss the message, but it kept creeping back in my consciousness. Somehow, my physical fitness regimen, my turning thirty-five, and my new life with Charlotte were all creating a bridge that I was crossing.

During the last week in August, I decided to take a three day solo trip to the White Mountains of New Hampshire. This would be my own self-designed retreat. For whatever I was supposed to do I would return to a spot that Charlotte and I had found the previous summer.

Packing light for the trip, I took a small tent, a sleeping bag, camping stove, trail mix, and beans, and the Bowie knife. On a whim, I got Zlavik's bow and arrows that Nancy had given me as a parting gift. Charlotte threw me her most fetching grin as I left. "I will miss you, be sure to keep your distance from those wood nymphs. They may want that new body of yours."

I laughed at her humor and good grace. "I'll be true to you, but I cannot be responsible for what happens in my dream state."

"A clever answer from a horny woodsman."

We both laughed, then embraced.

I was off.

I got to the site in late afternoon after a two hour hike. Instinct had guided me back; there were no trails. I smiled, noticing the campfire stones and the rock pyramid that Charlotte and I had made. There were no signs of anyone else's presence since we'd left.

The spot was a t-shaped miniature canyon with fifteen-foot granite walls that encircled a small shallow brook-fed pool. At the back of the canyon was a sandy beach where I pitched my tent. Charlotte and I had called it our Eden. I unpacked my gear and lit a fire on the stone fireplace. I sat and scanned the area. Memories of the time here with Charlotte were coming back.

I ate my Campbell's beans after bathing in the cold water. It was dusk and I was feeling restless. Later, some of the night noises made me uneasy, but I drifted off to sleep.

I awoke the next morning. The day was warm and I stripped to a pair of cutoff shorts and sneakers. Feeling 'native,' I strapped Martin's Bowie knife and sheath to my waist. I started laughing, like a twelve-year-old on his first overnight camping trip. For the first half of the day I hummed, whistled and sang to myself as I puttered and played in the canyon. Later I found some red clay and smeared streaks on my cheeks and chest. I found a feather which I stuck into the side of my hair. Half-Indian and half-Huck Finn, I sauntered about my campsite for the next hour making up Indian chants and whooping.

I caught sight of my image in the pond. I recalled the famous 1890's photograph by Edward Curtis called "The Pool—Apache." A lone Indian stood with only his loincloth on in solitude by a river, with the forest behind him. He was the archetypal primeval man. My own reflection fused with the picture's image.

The rest of the afternoon was spent napping, writing in my journal, and rebuilding the campfire stones. Later, I lay back against a moss covered tree stump. I fell asleep and had a short dream about Martin being with me again. We were near Zlavik's house searching for the giant wolf. We could smell it, and hear it move through the brush, but somehow it kept eluding us.

I awoke feeling a tightness in my chest. Something was off.

Chapter 31

I decided to move my position from the stump to a place ten feet away where I could face the entrance. I sat Indian style and began a scan of the canyon. I kept reassuring myself that nothing was there, but I felt an alarm bell inside start to vibrate.

My defenses broke when a sulphur-like smell assailed my nostrils. Every hair on my arms, legs, and neck, rose up. My stomach clenched and my throat muscles began closing and tightening like someone was choking me. A whump, whump sound heaved upward in my chest.

Something was approaching the entrance. I still saw nothing, yet the sulphur-like smell suffused the air.

Then I saw it. A giant, black wolf--looking more like a Bengal tiger--stood at the entrance. The animal's dark hair glistened in the afternoon sun and the thick neck and huge head and its yellow eyes with the large dark pupils mesmerized me.

I remembered David's explanation that it would either kill Zlavik or those he loved. I saw the end of an arrow sticking out several inches from the wolf's chest. This was the wolf that David had shot.

Its mouth was open wide, baring all its teeth, front fangs dripping saliva. I thought for a moment I saw a kind of grin in the creature's expression and could even hear a sound of glee in the deep savage growling. These were the same sounds I'd heard in my backyard. This creature had been stalking me, on and off, for over three years.

The growling increased. The wolf seemed to be savoring its purpose as it stood fifty feet from me blocking the only way out. The walls behind me were too jagged and high--I was trapped. The animal waited a moment, and began to advance towards me. It let out a loud howl that roared through the small area like a compressed ball of thunder.

The wolf moved through the shallow pool of water, and stopped at about thirty feet.

I felt like a cornered prey wanting it to be over. I recalled the frozen feeling I'd had when Martin had been mauled, and like then, I kept reminding myself this wasn't real. The panic shifted. I entered a hazy dream world that had no wolf. Time was spinning me far away.

However, the peace of the new reality was interrupted by the sound of a major circuit switch being thrown on. Something was changing inside. There was new energy coming up through my spine and spiraling out in all directions. The change was an affirming, joyous surge that was invading every vein and artery. A Tsunami wave of adrenalin had released itself.

I stood and made direct eye contact with the wolf, and surprising myself, I advanced three steps towards my enemy. Another awareness glided in: my two brothers--although in different forms--were now with me. I could feel Zlavik's presence on my left side and Martin's on my right. Their allegiance was unconditional.

All my senses: sight, hearing, smell, touch were super-heightened. Old ways were coming back: I would know how to fight the wolf.

I took another three steps, entering into the shallow pool. Twenty feet now separated me from the wolf. The creature let loose growls that rumbled for a full minute. His black gums were flared back, exposing glistening teeth.

Once more I felt the presence of my two brothers. Martin closed in on the right as Zlavik moved in on the left. The corners of my triangle tightened as I became the moving point of an invisible but potent phalanx.

The wolf hesitated sensing the presence of the new energies. I took another step. Once more he released a series of growls, each one flowing into the other, until the rocky canyon was a cauldron of thundering echoes. The animal's muscles started to twitch and ripple as he prepared to hurl himself at me.

Inside of me, I could feel old iron doors clang open. Once more I was the hairy man in the tree who had bayed at the moon. His fierceness for blood was the equal of the wolf's. I reached into the water and felt a huge jagged rock, which I picked up. I felt pleasure as I made loud guttural noises at the creature. Instinct became king as I raised the rock over my head and heard, the warrior: *Kill it!*

I hurled the rock at the wolf. I saw a large, red gash appear on the wolf's right shoulder as it fell to the ground.

I removed the Bowie knife from its sheath. I remembered how I'd been frozen with the knife when my brother died. Not now, I was awake and I would use the weapon to dispose of the wolf. Martin's death would be avenged. I held the knife straight out in the air with my right hand extended and raced through the water to finish the job. Two steps later, propelled by my own weight and speed, I slid on the moss-covered bottom hurling myself face down into the water.

I was laying in about three inches of water, dazed. I could feel dozens of cuts and scratches all over my face, chest, and legs. I pushed myself up, resting first on my knees then wobbled to an upright position. Worst of all I'd lost the Bowie knife.

I observed the condition of the wolf, whose eyes were on me. The animal raised itself to its feet and limped back to the shore.

Good, I thought. I've weakened it.

The wolf lay down on all four legs and faced me. I was standing up in the water still bleeding. The wolf lowered its head between its paws and made a series of low, strange humming noises. I moved back in the water looking for another rock that I could fling.

There were none. I kept watching the wolf. Ripples of energy began pulsing through him in increasing waves. The humming noise appeared to be some kind of self-healing, regeneration ritual. His muscles continued to contract and release underneath his fur as the sound continued. Several minutes later, the wolf stood up on all fours--he had recovered his power.

"Damn!"

I kept backing up into deeper water. Panic returned. I caught my throat muscles tightening, but countered by focusing on my breath count. The wolf pawed at the dirt. Now, he was entering the water, coming straight for me.

Breathing slow, I kept eye contact. Slowly, I sensed the corners of my triangle returning. The trinity of brothers was still present.

The wolf was, again, emitting its savage growls. It took several steps then launched itself for my throat. I threw up my right forearm to block him as his massive weight crushed me into the water. I heard the crunching of bones and saw blood in the water as the animal's teeth tore into my right forearm. I was pulled into a tunnel and my body was being left behind. I was going far away where no wolf existed. Only a faint voice could be heard repeating a message.

'Remember your soccer kick.' The voice was Martin's.

'Now.'

I opened my eyes and spotted my opening. The wolf's huge testicles were exposed. I grabbed with my only hand and flipped the wolf to his side.

I focused all my remaining strength into my right foot, I let the kick release itself with a force like a catapult heaving a boulder. A mournful bellow filled the canyon, as the creature rolled back and forth, it's body writhing in a series of violent spasms.

Still feeling dizzy, I managed to stand and hobble the thirty feet back to my tent. My right arm was bleeding, heavily, from the puncture wounds. I got a T-shirt and with my left hand and teeth, managed to make a crude tourniquet.

I watched the wolf get up, whimpering in pain, as he limped with small steps back to his spot. He turned, faced me, and snarled.

CHAPTER 32

I heard the wolf begin his piercing, humming noise that had reincarnated him earlier. He was hunched down—again—on all fours, facing me, his head on his paws, eyes closed. It was as though his whole form was in supplication to whatever deity had spawned him.

I watched as the waves of energy began rippling under his fur, and I could feel the panic return. I felt faint from the blood loss, and my right arm was useless. My entire body was battered, and the wolf was recreating himself anew.

I heard a voice. This time it was Zlavik. *Do your breath count.* I sat down on a small rock facing the wolf. Slowly, in the nose and out the mouth...only the breath. Several minutes went by and I was clearer.

Something new was happening. My brothers, one on each side, were touching me and creating twin currents of energy. Together they completed a circuit with me as the connecting arc. Adrenalin was pumping--again.

Allen, use the bow and arrow. Zlavik spoke.

I went to the tent and pulled out the forgotten bow and one arrow.

The wolf was standing on all fours. He had his eyes closed and was still making the humming noise--except softer. His strength was close to normal.

A warm air current glided back and forth over my injured right forearm. Heat flowed throughout the area. I knew it was Zlavik performing a healing ritual. I would have enough strength to release the arrow.

The wolf entered the water in slow motion. His eyes fixed on me. A new and deeper round of growls deafened me with their din.

I stood, placed the arrow in the bow, and stretched the weapon to its max. The corners of my triangle moved closer as I aimed the arrow at the approaching creature.

Aim for the old arrow--you must split it.

The wolf stopped at about twenty feet, and for the first time acted hesitant.

I screamed. "Come and get your arrow."

A full minute went by as we each remained motionless, scanning the other for movement.

My body started to shake and tremble and then merge into the unity of the breath and the taut bow.

The wolf opened its mouth baring all its teeth and catapulted itself towards me. At the same time, I released my arrow. It flew like a heat seeking missile tearing deep into the shank of the old arrow.

The wolf landed at my feet, emitting one last mega howl as I jumped back. I was motionless as the twitching and convulsions of the animal went on for several minutes before I heard the death rattle.

The fight had sent me spinning back to a forgotten past. There were rituals to perform. I knelt down alongside the creature, placing my hand on its head. I prayed briefly to whatever reality he had come from. I'd taken the life of a fellow warrior. The sanctity of our combat needed to be honored.

I walked over and retrieved the Bowie knife and returned to the fallen animal. I bent down and used the knife in a saw-like fashion, severing its head from the body. It took several minutes to hack through the thick vertebrae and strong neck muscles, but my hands remembered—I'd done this before.

Putting my right foot on the wolf's back, I lifted the decapitated head by the ears--holding it high over my head.

I began circling the creature, showing off the head to my assembled but invisible ancestors. I started muttering unfamiliar words and phrases as I danced around the carcass. My tongue remembered the ancient language.

The sounds then switched to cries and yells, as I stopped at each of the four directions. Long, burgundy rivulets of blood were dripping down on my chest from the raised, decapitated head. I circled and spun fast around the creature's body like a whirling dervish. During all this time I kept sensing the unseen tribes as I displayed my trophy.

Breathless, I stopped the dance and returned the head to its position. Next, I began smearing the dripped blood that was on my face and chest until I was covered in the color of birth.

I began a pounding on my chest letting the rhythm and cadence emerge on their own. A new series of cries and yells emerged. The sounds continued and the canyon was filled with the sounds of healing and rebirth.

Emptied, I fell down alongside the wolf, but, I was not done. New guides had appeared and were using me as a conduit. My lower body began moving and twitching as a series of sharp spasms shot up my legs into my upper body. I moaned as the spasms sprang into a succession of wave-like shocks. My arms and legs were flailing, my back arched.

There was a flash of silver light...I was Martin being ripped apart by the junkyard dogs...and another flash...I was Zlavik writhing in the agony of his grand-mal seizure. I lost consciousness, lying alongside the wolf.

I awoke, later that afternoon, aching everywhere from my throbbing right arm, to the cuts and bruises of my fall. I felt like I'd fallen from the moon to the earth. I managed to stand up and see my reflection in the pool. The image was repulsive: I was covered in a caked afterbirth of dirt and blood and there was a terrible stench.

Stripping off my clothes, I entered the deepest part of the water and sat down. The shock of the cold water helped to clear me. For several minutes I washed and rubbed the caked layers with grainy sand and watched as the old layers were taken away. I closed my eyes and breathed for awhile.

I stood and saw the new reflection: naked and reborn.

Returning to the campsite, my right arm was beginning to throb, so I downed two aspirin from my first-aid kit. I stuffed the rest of the camp gear into my backpack. I dried myself, putting on a clean jersey and pants.

Before I left the site, I sat down and leaned back against the soft, moss-covered stump. My chest felt lighter and the metal band that had encased my chest for over twenty years was gone.

I closed my eyes and rode my breaths.

In the quiet, I realized I'd completed the third task.

About the Author

Peter A. Jarrett is an educator with a wealth of life experiences. He has been a high school English and social studies teacher as well as a high school guidance counselor. He also has been an adjunct faculty member at a variety of colleges and universities, including: Antioch, Golden Gate, University of Southern New Hampshire and Franklin Pierce College. He holds a Doctorate in Education from Vanderbilt University.

The novel "Zlavik" reflects Peter's interdisciplinary interests in religion, philosophy, politics, and psychology. He believes that our quest for meaning is ultimately found as we open ourselves to experience the transcendent in our daily lives.

Printed in the United States
80630LV00004B/223-261

9 781420 852219